"Why did you ask me to marry you?"

Thea raised her eyes in expectation, but all Marcus said was, "I told you."

"That doesn't answer my question," she replied quietly. "I'm green and inexperienced—that's really what you meant, wasn't it? You felt you couldn't take advantage of me, right?"

"I guess that's what it boils down to," he replied dryly.

Thea shook her head. "But why marriage?" she asked.

"Would you have settled for less?" he asked her bluntly.

"Not if you mean what I think you mean," she snapped indignantly.

The shrug of his shoulders was eloquent. "Are you honestly telling me," Thea exclaimed impatiently, "that you were prepared to tie yourself down for life on a whim—just because, b-because...." She couldn't go on.

Marcus's eyes opened wide. "Who said it was for life?"

JANE CORRIE
is also the author of these
Harlequin Romances

Pirates' Lair

by

JANE CORRIE

Harlequin Books

TORONTO • LONDON • LOS ANGELES • AMSTERDAM
SYDNEY • HAMBURG • PARIS • STOCKHOLM • ATHENS • TOKYO

Original hardcover edition published in 1980
by Mills & Boon Limited

ISBN 0-373-02413-4

Harlequin edition published July 1981

CHAPTER ONE

THEA JOHN gazed out of her bedroom window on to the sun-drenched beach directly below her. She could have been gazing at an arctic landscape, for there was no warmth in her heart, only a block of ice where her heart should have been.

She then glanced back at the small clock on her bedside table which told her that Marcus would be picking her up in precisely fifteen minutes' time.

Her breath was drawn in sharply at the thought of what she would have to tell him. It was no use putting it off, or pretending that what happened last night simply hadn't happened, or that Sapphire had acted on a jealous impulse and made up that awful story she had told her when Marcus had dropped her back at her hotel after their engagement party.

Her eye caught her reflection in the wall mirror and she nodded grimly at her image. 'You didn't really believe a man like that could fall for you, did you?' she said bitterly to her reflection.

She moved hastily away from the window as if by this one single movement she could blot out the memory of Sapphire's triumphant black eyes as she had sent Thea's world crashing around her, and sat down slowly on the bed. It would be a long time before she would be able to get that scene out of her mind, if ever.

It was two months now since she had come to St

Thomas, in the U.S. Virgin Islands. Two months since she had learnt of the death of her brother whom she had travelled from England to join.

Thea's soft lips twisted at the thought and her heart felt as heavy as lead, but she made herself go over it all again, as if by driving the knife into her wound, she could come to terms with this second blow fate had dealt her.

She remembered stepping off the plane on to a sun-splashed runway and looking eagerly around for any sign of Michael, who knew what time she would be arriving and would be certain to be there to greet her.

Her glance strayed to the magnificent emerald ring she wore on her third finger; the green fire of the stone flashed back an answering echo and she swallowed hastily. So like Marcus's eyes, she thought painfully. He had green eyes, and she had seen them flash just like that when aroused to fury by a thoughtless comment made by a jealous contender for his attention, and who only succeeded in getting herself barred from the intimate circle of his close friends.

She stirred restlessly; her thoughts were wandering and she must collect them. There had been no Michael to meet her, but a tall exceedingly good-looking man with chestnut hair bleached blond by the sun, who had introduced himself as Michael's boss and suggested that he take her somewhere where he could talk to her.

When she followed his tall well-groomed figure out to a sleek car waiting in the airport car park after claiming her luggage, she had no idea of the stark news that awaited her of her brother's death the previous evening in a car smash.

Thea's soft lips clamped together. Whatever she accused Marcus of now, she could not deny that he had helped her through that black period of her life. Even though it had turned out that he had a particular reason for his concern, but she could forgive him that; what she couldn't forgive was what had happened afterwards.

Sapphire's cold voice reached through to her again as it had done before, like a recording now imprinted on her brain. 'Enjoy yourself while you may,' she had said, almost spitting the words out. 'You're in for a shock if you think he's in love with you.'

Thea had not been too concerned about this vitriolic attack from Sapphire Durley. She was in love with Marcus, and from what Thea had been able to gather about the past she had been around some time. Thea had reasoned that it couldn't have been serious on Marcus's part or he would have married her, and a determined woman will always place more emphasis on small inconsequential happenings to further her cause. She had replied in a light manner, showing Sapphire that she had failed if she had wanted to upset her. 'Do you think he'll leave me standing at the altar, then?' she had asked.

Sapphire's eyes had glinted even fiercer at this. 'Better for you if he did!' she had retorted bitterly. 'But don't worry, he'll go through with it all right. The way he sees it, he's got to!'

Thea stared back at Sapphire as a cold feeling played down her spine. 'Oh, now what makes you say that?' she asked as casually as she was able. 'He doesn't strike me as the kind of man who would do anything he didn't want to do.'

'That's as much as you know!' Sapphire had snapped back at her. 'And you know nothing! Anyone with a grain of sense would have seen why he's marrying you. You can take it from me that Marcus isn't the marrying type—and I ought to know!' she tacked on bitterly. 'But none of this would have occurred to you, would it? You're living in a fairy story, pet, and they went out of fashion years ago. What do you know about your brother's death?' she suddenly shot out at Thea. 'Or were you so caught up with Marcus's wooing that you didn't give yourself time to think about it?' she sneered.

Thea's shocked grey eyes gave Sapphire the satisfaction she had been seeking. 'What exactly do you mean?' she whispered. 'What has Michael's death to do with me and Marcus?'

'Everything!' replied Sapphire gratingly, yet with a certain amount of triumph in her voice. 'If Marcus hadn't sent for him at that time of night, he wouldn't have died. It's as simple as that.'

Thea's bewildered senses grappled with this cold fact, then she rallied enough to say, 'But it wasn't Marcus's fault he crashed. He just took a bend too fast,' she ended lamely.

Sapphire nodded grimly. 'Which he wouldn't have done if he hadn't been half-cut,' she added significantly, and at Thea's still bewildered look, she said impatiently, 'Look, the way Marcus sees it, he should have known that Michael would be at that party. He did know, of course, but he wanted to see those plans. He works all hours himself and is inclined to think that everybody else does, and when Marcus commands he expects quick results.'

Thea shook her head as if trying to clear it, not yet able to grasp the significance behind Sapphire's words. 'I still don't see——' she began.

'Don't, or don't want to see,' Sapphire cut in savagely. 'For heaven's sake grow up! Marcus has a chip on his shoulder about Michael's death, and here's his little sister who's just lost her only relative.' She gave an offhand shrug. 'He could have made sure that you got adequate compensation, but oh no, not Marcus. That wasn't enough for him and his king-sized conscience! He had to do the grand thing and marry you. That way he'd pay for his thoughtlessness—and I mean pay,' she tacked on, working herself up to a frenzy. 'You're not Marcus's type, honey, and never will be. Sure, he's given you a ring, the biggest and best he could find, and believe me, nothing's going to be too good for you. You'll have a beautiful house, lovely clothes, in fact everything a girl could want, except his love, and you'll never have that. Take a good look in the mirror at yourself, honey. I know his taste, and believe me, the country cousin type leaves him cold, but he's experienced enough never to let you know his true feelings, and that underneath it all he feels sorry for you!'

Thea had taken a good look at herself in the mirror after Sapphire had stormed out of her apartment. Through tear-dimmed eyes she could well see what Sapphire had meant. Her clear grey eyes had gone critically over her small elfin features, noting the generous mouth that was now clamped in a line to prevent it trembling, and her small upturned nose that made her look younger than her twenty-two years. Her red hair was nothing to set the world on fire about, either, for it was a dark red that only showed its best points when the glints of the sun caught it.

She turned slightly sidewise. As for her figure— well, she hadn't one! Her five feet two height and slim nature had nothing in the way of feminine curves, and recalling Sapphire's voluptuous curves and magnificent long legs, plus her dark lovely gypsy-type looks, she closed her eyes and hurried away from the mirror.

Her breath caught on a raw-sounding sob. She was only putting off the inevitable; she didn't want to think about all those other things Sapphire had said. Her hands clenched into small fists. Sapphire had a reason to make trouble for her, she loved Marcus and was making a fight to keep him free from any other entanglement.

Her small white teeth clenched together. She wouldn't believe a word of it! It wasn't true— Marcus wouldn't—she caught her breath. What was the use? It was true, every word of it! It made sense of so much that she hadn't been able to understand. She had not been allowed to dwell in the shadows of grief; Marcus had seen to that. Marcus, she thought, had seen to everything. Even this flatlet belonged to him, for it was part of the huge complex of holiday flats that he owned, and that her brother Michael had designed additional units for, the plans of which he had been bringing to Marcus the night he died.

Thea sat on her bed. She had never felt so vulnerable in her life before, or so foolish. She ought to have known that a man like Marcus Conan would not have looked twice at a slight boyish-looking girl like her, not without a reason, and she now knew that reason.

'Hi! Are you ready, honey?' Marcus's voice reached through Thea's musings and she gave a start, then got up slowly from the bed and went out into the small lounge of the flatlet.

At the sight of his tall lean figure dressed in casual white polo-necked sweater and navy blue cords, her heart missed a beat, and somehow she managed to avoid meeting those green eyes of his as she announced calmly, 'I'm not going, Marcus.'

Once it would never have occurred to her to wonder at his casual greeting, but now her eyes were open. It was hardly the way a lover greeted his beloved, was it? she thought bitterly.

His reply was typical too. 'Okay, sweetheart, so we give the beach party a miss. What have you in mind? A laze on the beach, maybe?' he asked, sounding amused—as if humouring a child, she thought angrily.

Her anger dispersed as quickly as it had arisen. She had no one but herself to blame for what had happened. 'As a matter of fact, I want to talk to you,' she said quietly, her candid grey eyes meeting his for the first time since his arrival. Then with the same quiet deliberation, she took the ring off her third finger and laid it down on the small occasional table beside her, and felt rather than saw Marcus's hard stare at her action. 'I don't feel it's right to go ahead with——' she faltered slightly, then carried on more firmly. 'I don't want to be a salve to your conscience, Marcus. I just wish you'd been honest with me from the start.' She couldn't go on, there was no need to; he must know what she was getting at, she thought miserably.

His reply of, 'I'd like that put a little more plainly, please,' startled her, and she knew that he was going to see the whole wretched thing through to the bitter end. He might have spared her that, she thought bleakly.

'Do you want it in capitals?' she queried bluntly, her fine eyes meeting his hooded ones. 'I know the reason why you want to marry me. It's because of Michael, isn't it? Because you feel responsible for what happened. Didn't it ever occur to you that I'd find out the truth one day? And how I'd feel about our marriage?' she demanded bleakly.

'By that time it wouldn't have made any difference,' Marcus replied harshly. 'I'd make sure of that.'

One part of Thea acknowledged the bitter truth that he had not attempted to deny her charge, the other part recognised the meaning behind his last words and a slight flush stained her features. 'I'm slow, I'll admit,' she said quietly, 'but not that slow.' She forced herself to remain calm as she met his determined eyes. 'I don't blame you for what happened to Michael and I fail to see why you should blame yourself. He always drove faster than he should have done. I suppose it would have happened one day—the accident, I mean,' she added wearily. 'Can't we leave it at that? I see no point in arguing about it. I just want to say I'm grateful for all you've done for me since——' she swallowed. 'Well, anyway, thanks,' she ended lamely.

'Are you turning me down because of that?' demanded Marcus, his green eyes piercing Thea's grey ones. 'In which case it's pretty obvious that you do blame me.'

Thea gasped. She didn't seem to have got through to him at all. He was determined to use her as a sop to his conscience, and she was just as determined to stop him. 'It's not that,' she said quickly, only just stopping herself from shouting the words at him. 'If only you'd told me how you felt—but you didn't, did you? You could have told me that he was on his way to you with those plans you wanted to see the night of the accident. There could have been only one reason why you didn't.' She took a deep breath. 'As I said, eventually I would have found out about that and—' her voice trembled, 'several other things that it's not necessary to go into now.'

'Care to tell me the name of your informant?' Marcus asked, his eyes now narrowed to a slit.

Thea shook her head decisively. 'No,' she said abruptly.

'I see,' Marcus replied through thin lips. 'So—where do we go from here?'

'We go nowhere,' Thea got out through clenched teeth. 'From now on I'm on my own. I'm quite capable of looking after myself. Michael was often away abroad, and I didn't accompany him, I only came here because he'd decided to settle here.' She swallowed. 'I haven't had time to work anything out yet, but no doubt I'll come up with something,' she added firmly.

'You'll go back to the U.K., will you?' Marcus asked, almost abstractedly.

Again there was a decisive shake of the head from Thea. 'I've nothing to go back for,' she said simply. There was no self-pity in her voice. 'I cut all my ties when I left. I shall try and get a work permit here and find a job,' she announced quietly.

'There'll be no problem there,' Marcus replied slowly, 'about the job, either. I'll be able to fix you up with something in that line.'

'No, thank you!' retorted Thea, feeling in the middle of some sort of play and just saying her lines, closing her mind to the plain but bald fact that not once had Marcus attempted to make her change her mind about marrying him. 'I said I was on my own, and I meant just that,' she told him, and glanced around the lounge. 'I shall move out as soon as I find some other accommodation, but thank you for offering to help me,' she added, not able to disguise the bitterness in her voice.

Marcus stood looking at her for what seemed an age, and Thea wanted to scream at him to get out of the flat and out of her life. His hard gaze left her and rested on the ring. 'Take it,' she said in a low voice, not able to look at him. 'You'll probably find some use for it.'

She saw his firm lips straighten at this. 'Keep it,' he said abruptly. 'You may find a use for it yourself one day,' and on that terse direction he walked out of the flat.

Thea waited until she heard his car start up, then walked shakily back to the bedroom. At first she knew a bitter-sweet relief that she had been able to extricate herself from what could have been a disastrous situation. She could have found out the truth a day before her wedding, and the consequences of standing Marcus up would have been too awful to contemplate. She would have gone ahead rather than let him suffer such an indignity, particularly as his reason for marrying her had been purely to protect her future by taking over Michael's role.

She shook her head dumbly. He had gone the wrong way about it. She would have been grateful for any help he would have offered her. He hadn't had to pretend that he loved her. Her tears fell thick and fast, and were a kind of release for her. She had not shed one tear after Sapphire's virulent exposure of the true reason why Marcus was marrying her.

After indulging in the luxury of tears, Thea slipped through to the bathroom and bathed her swollen eyes. It was time she pulled herself together and thought about the future.

First she had to apply for a work permit, she told herself firmly, in order to evade the memories that threatened to swamp her and engulf her back in the past again. Next she had to find a job. She was a trained dental assistant, or had been before Michael had decided to pull up his roots and settle abroad. There were bound to be some dentists on the island, she told herself stoutly, and if she couldn't get a job in that profession, then she would take a receptionist job in one of the hotels on the island. She had heard there were nearly always vacancies in that capacity. Oh, there were plenty of job opportunities, she was sure. It only required getting the necessary permit for work.

She knew that she would have to be seconded by someone resident on the island, and wished miserably that she hadn't been so adamant on refusing help from Marcus as she didn't really know anyone else to ask for the necessary endorsement. If it came to that, she didn't really know Marcus, she thought bleakly. Sapphire's cutting remark that she didn't know anything was proving absolutely correct.

Her mind went back to the day she had first met Marcus and he had told her about Michael.

Events after that were rather hazy. Thea could only remember that Marcus had given her no time to sit around and mope. First he had installed her in the flatlet that was part of the hotel complex that he owned, and only a stone's throw away from the main hotel area where he lived and worked. She had been taken out each evening for meals at small exclusive restaurants, and after a fortnight had passed, taken to parties that brought her in contact with many of his friends.

By the time a month had slipped by Marcus became more attentive towards her. Then had come the evening that he had kissed her goodnight, a light feathery kiss on her lips that had left her with stars in her eyes. The same would happen each night after that, and Thea would find herself eagerly awaiting their partings and the light but very acceptable kiss he would give her.

Looking back to that moment in time, she simply could not understand why she had not realised that Marcus was not in love with her. At no time had he said he was, but, moonstruck, Thea had never sought any such confirmation. She was too much in love with this handsome man who had singled her out for his attention.

She closed her eyes and recalled the night that he had proposed to her, and her stunned but delighted reaction to his blunt, 'Marry me, Thea.' That was all that he had said, there had been no further embellishment, or declaration of his love for her.

Thea sighed. What a crass idiot she was! She had been indulging in a daydream. The man she had fallen in love with was part of that dream, because he didn't really exist. Michael had once described Marcus as being the toughest boss he had ever encountered, adding that you had to be tough to survive in the jungle of commerce, but although he liked him well enough, he would not care to cross him. 'This is pirate country, my dear,' he had written, 'and I'm in the pirate's lair, so I'd better come up to scratch!'

Thea had smiled when she had read this, but all the same she had felt a tiny tug of worry and wished that he had not accepted the commission.

What Michael had said about Marcus made it very hard for Thea to reconcile the man she had come to know and the man Michael had described. He had certainly not sounded like the kind of man to take on the job of caring for his sister, even on the dictates of conscience.

When she had managed to reduce the swelling around her eyelids, she walked back into the lounge, and as her eyes caught the ring on the table, she winced. Its bright gleam seemed to leer at her from a distance and she hastily picked it up and put it away in the drawer of the bureau. Marcus's last words taunted her as she shut the drawer firmly. 'You may find a use for it yourself one day.'

Thea stared at the closed drawer. Did he mean she might need to sell it? she wondered miserably. She would never do that, but she did wish that he had taken it. It was a very valuable ring and she would feel uncomfortable while it was in her possession. It was not the type of ring one could wear for special occasions either, for it was bound to cause comment from some innocent person and would bring about a chain of memories Thea would rather not recall.

Her thoughts went back to Michael. He hadn't known Marcus at all, not really known him. There had been no piratical attitude towards her decision to back out of the engagement. He had not attempted to make her change her mind, and considering that they had only just celebrated their engagement it only went to show how considerate he was, and was surely a point in his favour, she thought sadly. Conscience or no, it must have been a blow to his ego.

Thea blinked suddenly. What was she doing? Trying to turn Marcus into a saint? It was her ego that had been bruised, not his. It would be her his friends would feel sorry for, not Marcus. He had probably grinned all the way back to the car and congratulated himself on his release.

Her soft mouth twisted. He had made the gesture, and surely that would be enough to settle his conscience. He must be thanking his lucky stars that he had got off so lightly, and she was glad she had not disappointed him.

How stupid of her not to have accepted his offer of help, she thought. He owed her that much, surely? There was nothing else she wanted of him, and she would take good care to keep out of his way as soon as she had found herself somewhere to stay, although there was little likelihood of seeing him in the future, as she wouldn't be moving in his exalted circles.

Thea felt much better after this. She had been a fool, but at least she could admit it, and if it hadn't been for Sapphire——

Her phone rang just as she was getting ready to go out in search of a local paper to scan the advertisement columns, looking for a job and for accommodation.

'I happen to know of a hotel that requires a receptionist,' Marcus's voice came over the line. 'That's if you're still of the same mind?' he queried softly.

It took a second or so for Thea to get her breath, and when she did she answered calmly enough. 'I'm still of the same mind. Where is the hotel?' she asked, telling herself that if it happened to be Marcus's hotel she would refuse.

His smooth reply soon dispersed this fear, as he told her which hotel it was, and its location.

Within a few minutes of Marcus's call, Thea rang the hotel and got herself an interview for the following morning. During the telephone conversation she had had with the manager, she had been asked her present address, and asked if she minded living in the hotel, as the work included shifts of duty and it was preferable for the staff to live in.

When Thea put the phone down a few minutes later she felt a sense of accomplishment. If she were successful in obtaining the job, it would automatically solve her next problem, that of finding somewhere to live.

The fact that it was Marcus who had told her about the job only convinced her that she had made the right decision. He was probably as anxious to get her settled and right out of his vicinity as she was to oblige.

CHAPTER TWO

BAY VIEW was one of several hotels situated on a hilltop overlooking the harbour, with lovely views of Charlotte Amalie, and was about five miles out of town, up a steep winding road.

Although large, it was nothing like the huge complex of Marcus's hotel, and as Thea had looked up at it as the taxi that was taking her to the hotel for the interview began the upward ascent towards the large white cemented building that sat perched on the top of the hillside, much like an eagle on its nest, she found herself hoping that she would be successful in her quest for a job.

Half an hour later she was being shown the room she would be sharing with the girl who had taken her on a tour of the hotel.

Pauline Foster was a cheerful, nice-looking blonde American girl whose uncle managed the hotel, and as Thea listened to her animated conversation, she congratulated herself on her good fortune in not only having secured the job she needed so badly, but sharing accommodation with such a pleasant personality as Pauline.

'There's really nothing to it,' Pauline said earnestly, after Thea had confessed that she knew nothing whatsoever about the job and how delighted she had been when told that the job was hers. 'All you have to remember is that our guests are on holiday and it's up to us to make their stay as

pleasant as possible. There'll be days when you
won't feel like smiling, but you'll have to force yourself!' She had grinned at Thea as she said this. 'I'll
try to wangle it that you're on duty at the same time
as I am, and I can show you the ropes.'

Thea was surprised that there should be more
than two receptionists. The hotel boasted forty
rooms and everything seemed to be smooth-running,
but she had forgotten the shifts, as Pauline reminded
her.

'There's always someone on duty,' she explained.
'There's a day shift and an evening shift. You won't
do the evening shift yet awhile, not until you've got
the hang of things.'

All Thea had to do now was to move in, which
meant that she had to go back to the flatlet and
collect her luggage, for it had been arranged that
she should start work the following day.

Back at the flat she packed her clothes into her
suitcases and tried not to think of what might have
been, but concentrated on her future, a future without Marcus's guiding hand.

Only when everything was packed did she feel a
pang of uncertainty about what to do about
Marcus. She ought to ring him and tell him that
she had been successful in getting the job, but the
chances were that he wouldn't be in his office. He
preferred to be on the move, and hated having to be
tied down. She gave a light shrug. Well, she could
try anyway, and if he was out she would have to
drop a note into the hotel on her way out.

To her surprise he was in the office, and she gave
him the message, adding with as much enthusiasm
as she could muster, for the sound of his deep voice

had brought unwelcome reminiscences to her, 'I'm going to like the job, I'm sure.'

'How about a celebration lunch, then?' Marcus asked.

Thea swallowed. 'I don't think so, Marcus,' she replied slowly. 'I've things to do,' she added lamely. Seeing him again would not help her to come to terms with her new future.

'What things?' Marcus demanded autocratically.'

For a moment she was stumped for an answer, then she rallied with, 'There are things I must get. I'm starting work tomorrow, remember.'

'So we'll go on a shopping tour,' Marcus said quietly. 'I'll pick you up in fifteen minutes.'

'No, you won't!' Thea said hastily, hating the way he had assumed the role of guardian again, as if she were a little girl he must provide for. 'I said I was on my own now and I meant it. Try to understand, please. I'm very grateful for all you've done for me, and I'll never forget you,' she ended on a cracked note.

'Sounds like an obituary,' Marcus said dryly.

'Oh, I didn't mean it like that,' Thea cried. 'You know I didn't. Don't make things difficult for me, please!'

There was a long silence at Marcus's end after this, and Thea, feeling the tension and unable to bear it a moment longer, said timidly, 'Marcus?'

'Very well,' he replied slowly. 'If that's really what you want.'

'It's what I want,' she told him firmly, feeling her nails biting into the soft flesh of her palm.

'Good luck with the job,' Marcus said softly, before he put the receiver down. 'You know where to find me.'

Thea replaced her receiver with a feeling of finality bordering on grief for the loss of a loved one. Marcus's comment on an obituary had been very near the truth, as far as she was concerned anyway. With Marcus out of her life, her dreams would die. She straightened up slowly and walked to her cases—the taxi should be there any moment—and picked them up and took them to the door of the flatlet. Somehow she would manage to make a new life for herself; she had to.

The next few days were busy ones for Thea, and gave her no time to mope on what might have been. At the end of a week she was sufficiently able to cope with an influx of guests without having Pauline at her side to watch over her, and to answer the various questions the guests might ask, either about accommodation or places of interest to visit on the island.

The work was entirely to her liking. Pauline's presence helped her over her first few hazardous days, and from then on she started to enjoy her work, that was vastly different from her last employment where nervous patients had had to be soothingly led to the dental chair, and she was in no hurry to take up her previous occupation.

The expectancy and the gaiety of the holiday-makers was infectious, and it was only during her off-duty periods that she fell into a lethargic despondency. It was Pauline who helped her through that first week, but the weekend was an exceptionally lonely one for Thea, as Pauline's steady boy-friend was on leave from the luxury cruise ship

that had just docked in the harbour and where he
worked as a steward.

If Thea had had her way she would have much
preferred to work that weekend, for the thought of
Marcus intruded continually into her solitude, and
the thought that she only had to pick up the telephone and request his company, a request that she
knew he would not refuse, made things worse for
her.

The following Monday Marcus made a visit to
the hotel. Thea had been in the act of handing a
guest his keys when her eye had caught his familiar
figure entering the lobby, and she had turned away
hastily to look at something on the keyboard in
order to give herself time to compose herself before
she faced him.

It had been hard enough the last few days trying
to forget him. The work had helped, of course, but it
was not a remedy she could use in the long evenings
when Pauline had been out on a date, during which
time she had spent wondering which exotic woman
Marcus was entertaining, and invariably a vision of
Sapphire would appear before her.

When she turned back to the desk he was standing in front of her, his green eyes meeting her grey
ones. 'Well, how goes it?' he enquired solicitously.

Thea's gaze remained steady in spite of the
pounding of her heart at the close proximity of the
man she so desperately loved even though he was
not for her. 'Fine,' she replied noncommittally. 'It
took a day or so, but I think I've got the hang of it
now,' she added, wishing someone would come
for their keys or ask her a question, although the
chances were she wouldn't be able to answer it, but it

would give her a breathing space from those watchful eyes of his.

Marcus seemed to sense her discomfiture and gave her a smile that showed his strong white teeth. 'I was only passing, but I thought I'd look in to see how you were faring. You know where I am if you want anything,' he told her, and with another long searching look at her, he left.

'What did he want?' Pauline's voice broke through Thea's fixed concentration on the lobby door through which Marcus had just passed and she turned to look at Pauline.

'Marcus?' she asked.

Pauline blinked and gave her an odd look. 'Did you call him Marcus?' she demanded, 'or did I imagine it?'

Thea pulled herself away from her miserable musings. She had hoped that Marcus would ask her out for an evening, or suggest lunch or something. She hadn't seen him for a week now, and he could have suggested something, even though she would have to refuse, she thought contrarily. 'It's his name,' she replied quietly. 'He's Marcus Conan. He owns the Pirates' Cove hotel complex.'

Pauline gaped at her. 'Well, I know that, don't I?' she replied indignantly. 'He's on the board of directors of this place too. What I want to know is how you know him.'

It was Thea's turn to stare at Pauline. Marcus on the board of directors? So that was why she had got the job! It was all so simple when you knew the answers, she thought bitterly. 'Why shouldn't I know him?' she asked Pauline with raised brows, not willing to disclose just how well she did know Marcus.

Pauline continued to look at her. 'He doesn't exactly move in our circles, that's why,' she replied slowly. 'I don't know how you came across him, but I'd advise you to watch your step and don't go getting mooney over him or you'll get badly hurt. He's a gorgeous brute, I'll admit, but he's hard and wouldn't waste time on the likes of us.' Her eyes narrowed. 'It's rumoured that he's just got engaged to an English girl and it's the sensation of the century. He's not exactly the hearts and flowers type, more the cut-and-dried, take-it-or-leave-it brigade. Whoever she is, she must be quite something to have landed him.'

A thought then struck her and she looked back at Thea. 'You're English, aren't you? You wouldn't by any chance know her, would you? She's a newcomer to the island, like you,' she added hopefully.

Thea was in a quandary. If she told Pauline the truth she would ask endless questions, and she wanted to forget that part of her life. She hadn't really needed any confirmation of Sapphire's bald disclosures on why Marcus had proposed to her, but she was getting it all the same. It could surely do no harm to tell a white lie, and it would serve to explain Marcus's interest in her. 'As a matter of fact, I do,' she replied quietly.

Pauline's brown eyes widened a fraction as she exclaimed, 'Do you really! Is she pretty? Well, of course she'd have to be,' she half muttered to herself, 'probably beautiful,' she added wistfully.

Thea now wished that she had said that she didn't know the girl, but it was too late now and Marcus's visit had had to be explained as might other visits in the future. 'Well,' she edged, 'I wouldn't say she was all that pretty, Passable, perhaps.'

'Passable!' Pauline almost shrieked. 'You're not being catty, are you?' she queried suspiciously.

Thea swallowed. She badly wanted to smile, but the smile would have been a bitter one. 'I only met her on the plane coming over,' she explained carefully. 'I don't really know her, and you know what it's like on those long flights, it's so tiring,' she added lamely.

To her relief Pauline accepted this explanation, and an influx of guests who had just arrived on the morning flight from Miami excluded any further conversation.

For the rest of that week Thea and Pauline were on the first day shift from eight until two, and had the afternoons off. At first Pauline had suggested that she take Thea on a tour of the island, and this had been rather tricky for Thea, since Marcus had made a point of acquainting her with her new home during her first fortnight on the island, and as the island was only thirteen miles long and approximately three miles in width, it could be safely said that she had visited all the tourist haunts.

In the end, Thea had said something about her making a point of doing the rounds before she had looked for employment, but had no objection to going anywhere that Pauline thought would make a nice afternoon out, and Pauline had suggested a visit to the Mountain Top Hotel that sat high on the hill overlooking the beautiful Magens Bay, and from there to a laze on the beach.

Wearing comfortable jeans and a light cotton top, Thea stood beside Pauline, similarly dressed, and

looked out at the magnificent view spread out before
them on the balcony of the Mountain View hotel.
In the hazy distance could be seen the vague shapes
of the British Virgin Islands, and Pauline mentioned
this as they gazed out over the greeny-blue waters of
the bay, purplish coloured at the edges in the far
distance, denoting reefs of coral. The arms of the
island that formed the bay were clothed in verdant
green and looked like virgin forest land, and it was
hard to imagine that the island was in fact as small
as it was, for there were other bays further along the
coastline, all with the same golden beaches that
lured one away from the towns.

While they sipped at their banana daiquiris, the
hotel speciality, Pauline recounted a tale of how one
of their guests had unwisely refused to listen to the
local advice on the strength of the delicious drink
and had even made a bet with his fellow tourists on
the amount he could consume without side effects.
The result of this and his subsequent actions back at
the hotel, which included among other things a solo
performance of the dance of the seven veils, minus
the veils, in the hotel dining room, had not un-
naturally alarmed a few of the more timorous guests,
and caused a few others to seriously consider signing
the pledge!

These little amusing anecdotes helped Thea to
forget her previous visit there with Marcus, for she
had keenly felt his absence while she had stood
gazing out across the lovely bay, hearing once again
his strong deep voice recounting the past when
piracy was in its heyday, and the island provided a
haven for such awesome characters as Bluebeard,
Captain Kidd, and Captain Henry Morgan, to

name but a few of the men who had once struck terror in the hearts of those unfortunate enough to be waylaid on the high seas.

This had invariably invoked other memories, for she had recalled Michael's quip of being in 'pirate country' and had made her wish that she had stayed back at the hotel, or suggested somewhere else that they could go, but her low spirits had soon been dispelled by Pauline's vivacious chatter.

So the second week passed by pleasantly enough, and she was looking forward to a change of shift the following week when she would be on duty from two until ten. The late evening shift was taken over by the hotel porters who combined the checking in of guests and the carrying of luggage to the appointed rooms with no great difficulty, since few guests arrived during that period.

Pauline, however, was not so thrilled at the prospect of working until ten, for her John was still on leave, and would be until the end of the week. That, she had said, was the only complaint she had against the job, but you couldn't have everything, and considering the fact that this was only the second time in six months that her duties had clashed with John's off period, she didn't really have a complaint. She would be seeing him anyway in a fortnight's time.

Thea found that she enjoyed the afternoon shift better than the morning one, for apart from the fact that her evenings were taken care of, and the loneliness, not to mention her longing for Marcus's company, there was much more activity in the hotel lobby.

Around eight-thirty and onwards, the lobby

would be crowded with guests waiting to be picked
up by taxis, either going on an evening tour of the
island's night spots, or to a private dinner and
dance.

The women were invariably dressed in evening
wear, the dresses of various styles and colours giving
the select and rather formal reception area an
entirely new look that was refreshingly exhilarating
to Thea, and by the end of the week she was seriously considering asking to be put on the afternoon
shift permanently, as it would solve quite a few of
her problems. There would be no broken dates for
her to worry about, and with no further word from
Marcus, or visits from him, she could safely assume
that he had agreed to abide with her decision to go
her own way from now on.

By the Friday she had made up her mind to approach the manager with her request to be placed
permanently on the afternoon shift, but she had not
as yet told Pauline of her decision. Explaining the
reason why she wanted to do that shift was not
going to be easy, she thought, especially as Pauline
had tentatively suggested that John could bring
along a friend of his and they could make a foursome up next time he was on leave. It was going to
be even harder explaining that this was the last
thing Thea wanted, and was sure to evoke a few
unwanted questions from Pauline, whom she would
find looking at her in a kind of odd assessing way as
if she was an enigma to her, and wanted to be able
to place her in the right category.

As she did not want to hurt Pauline's feelings, she
resolved to tell her of her decision that evening
before she approached the manager with her re-

quest. By nine-thirty she would have ample opportunity of a private word with her, as the desk would be quiet by then.

Shortly after nine, however, an incident occurred that made her hastily revise her earlier thoughts of staying on the afternoon shift, when the last person she wished to see walked into the hotel.

Sapphire was just as lovely as she had remembered, and the scent of her heavy perfume reached over to Thea long before she reached the desk.

At first she did not see Thea, but approached the further end of the desk where Pauline stood. 'Tell Mr Bois I'm here,' she drawled in her husky voice, as if speaking to a bellboy.

Pauline's brown eyes took on an innocent look as she asked, 'And who shall I say wants to see him?'

Sapphire's black eyes snapped in fury. 'Miss Durley,' she snapped back at her.

Pauline gave a feigned hurt look as she rang through to her uncle, leaving a furious Sapphire to tap her heels while she waited, and it was then that she saw Thea, who was trying to look very busy checking the guest list.

'Well, well, look who's here,' she drawled. 'So you took my advice after all. How clever of you! I did ask Marcus where you'd got to, but he didn't seem to know,' she added slowly.

The last part was said in a manner that suggested that he hadn't cared either, and Thea caught the implication as Sapphire had intended that she should, but her steady grey eyes did not flinch as they met Sapphire's malicious ones.

'I think I'll accept Mr Bois's invitation, after all,'

she went on in a hard voice. 'It could prove interesting.'

Thea's gaze left Sapphire and rested on Pauline, whose dislike of the woman was plainly shown on her face as she said haughtily, 'My uncle will see you now. You know the way to the office, don't you?'

With a curt nod at Pauline and an airy wave in Thea's direction, Sapphire left for the manager's office.

Thea drew in a deep inward breath. What an objectionable woman she was, she thought, and could not understand her attitude at all. She was no threat to her now. She had got out of Marcus's life, and there could be no reason now for her to vent her spite on her.

Pauline's questioning brown eyes met Thea's dismayed ones and Thea looked away quickly. Now she would have to explain how she had met Sapphire, she thought miserably. 'I met her at a party,' she said lamely, in answer to Pauline's silent question.

'And got the wrong side of her, obviously,' Pauline replied dryly. 'Not that I'm surprised. The only friends that woman has are gentleman friends—she doesn't waste her smiles on women, especially the young and good-looking ones. She was one of the reasons I told you to steer clear of Marcus Conan, she's been hunting him for years. She mentioned him, didn't she?' she added thoughtfully. 'Why should she ask him where you were?' she demanded curiously.

Thea shrugged as casually as she was able to. 'Because Mr Conan took an interest in me, I suppose,'

was all she could come up with, but it served her
purpose.

'That figures,' Pauline commented dryly. 'That
would be enough to make her set the gun sights in
your direction. I wonder how she took the news of
his engagement to your friend,' she added with a
smile. 'Fit to chew nails, I should think! All that
ammunition wasted! If I didn't dislike her so, I'd
feel sorry for her,' she added with a wicked grin.

Thea was grateful for the intrusion of a few guests
at this point and hoped that that would be the end
of the conversation. She also hoped that Sapphire's
talk with the manager would last long enough for
her to escape out of her vicinity when her shift
ended in precisely fifteen minutes' time.

When Thea had thought that Sapphire's arrival
was a disturbing event, she had not known that
there was worse to come, for when Sapphire had
emerged from the manager's office only a short
while after she had gone in there, she had settled
herself down in one of the club chairs in the lobby
and giving Thea a tight smile had said, 'Don't
bother to ring for a taxi for me, I'm being picked
up.'

Pauline had given Thea a conspiratorial look
before they were again immersed in their duties, and
Thea was glad she was being kept busy, for she
could feel Sapphire's eyes upon her from where she
sat in the lobby with one elegant leg crossed over the
other, her tight figure-hugging evening dress with a
slit down the side giving any interested male a teas-
ing glimpse of a long, beautifully tanned leg.

A few minutes later came Thea's second shock of
the evening with the arrival of Marcus, who gave

her a quick acknowledging nod before he looked over at Sapphire and enquired if she were ready.

Thea did not wait to hear Sapphire's reply but deliberately took her time in searching for a guest's mail in the pigeonholes below the keyboard, and by the time she had located the mail and turned back to the desk Sapphire and Marcus had left.

Pauline's remarks on this little episode did not help either. 'Well, fancy that! I should have thought he'd be with his fiancée, wouldn't you?' she said. 'Still, I guess old habits die hard,' she added suggestively.

That was all she said, but it confirmed Thea's private thoughts on the matter. It had not taken long for Marcus to revert to his old way of life, and Sapphire had been part of that life, she thought bitterly.

For once she was pleased that Pauline would not be accompanying her back to their room, for John was waiting for her in the hotel bar, and Thea badly needed some solitude in which to recover from the unexpected events of the evening.

After a quick shower Thea got ready for bed, but knowing that she would not sleep slipped on her dressing gown and stood by the bedroom window gazing out on to the twinkling lights of the town. Where were Marcus and Sapphire now? she wondered. Had they gone back to Sapphire's flat——? She gave a small shudder, although the breeze coming in through the open window was not a cold one. Stop it! she whispered through clenched teeth. It was no concern of hers what they were doing.

She moved swiftly away from the window as if by the very action she could stem her thoughts, but it

was no use. Sapphire might not be a very nice
person, but there was no doubting the fact that she
was lovely. There was no doubting the fact that
Marcus was a man either, and that he obviously
found pleasure in her charms.

How could she have been so naïve? Thea asked
herself bitterly, as she recalled Marcus's feather-like
kisses, as if she had been a fragile article that would
splinter into a thousand pieces if roughly handled.
She then thought of the marriage that had almost
taken place. Poor Marcus, she thought bitterly, he
must have been dreading the event. Her small hands
clenched together. Well, she had saved him from
that unhappy involvement, and he was now free to
bestow his favours elsewhere.

Her eyes were bleak as she got into bed. She
couldn't imagine him kissing Sapphire like that. She
closed her eyes as the image of Marcus with
Sapphire in his arms floated before her. Why had
she to accept Mr Bois's invitation to sing at the
hotel? Pauline had said that they rarely put on any
entertainment in the hotel as there was plenty to be
had in Charlotte Amalie, and on the whole most of
the guests preferred to choose their own style of
entertainment.

Thea had never heard Sapphire sing, but by all
accounts she was a popular singer and much in
demand. Why then had she bothered about this
small hotel? There were plenty of hotels in and
around the town, with a larger guest contingent
than this one.

Her eyes flew open as the thought occurred to her
that perhaps she had known that Thea was there,
then she shook her head slowly. She couldn't have

known, she had been genuinely surprised to find her there. It must have been very gratifying for her to have Marcus pick her up like that, in full view of his ex-fiancée, she thought bleakly.

Thea bunched the pillows under her head. Marcus had known that she worked there, though, hadn't he? He had known where to pick Sapphire up. She frowned. Of course he couldn't have known that she would be on duty, she could still have been on the morning shift. Thea frowned as she recalled the way he had first glanced at her before looking at Sapphire, almost as if he expected to see her on duty. Again she shook her head. He couldn't have expected to see her, because if he had known her duty shift then what happened would have been a deliberate act on his part to cause her some embarrassment, and she couldn't believe that for one minute.

It all added up to one huge and very discomfiting coincidence, and Thea wondered miserably how long Sapphire's contract would run and whether she could possibly keep out of her way, and Marcus's too, as it was more than possible that he would make a habit of collecting Sapphire after the evening's performance.

One thing was certain, she would not seek a permanent job on the late afternoon shift, and if possible she would try to change her duty hours if Sapphire was still around when her next afternoon shift came around. If things got too tough, then she would move on, get a job on the other side of the island, without Marcus's help this time. In fact, she thought sleepily, it might be as well if she did that anyway. That way she could be sure of keeping her distance.

CHAPTER THREE

THEA's hope of avoiding Sapphire now that she was back on the morning shift proved to be wishful thinking on her part, for although a week had elapsed since she had seen her, her picture was displayed in the foyer announcing the fact that she would be entertaining the guests on the Saturday night, and every subsequent weekend after that for three months.

'Uncle says it's an experiment,' Pauline commented when she saw Thea looking at the poster shortly after it had been placed in the foyer. 'If it's successful, then he'll get in more evening entertainment. I only wish he'd chosen somebody else to start us off with,' she added, 'but I suppose everybody else was booked solid for the season. Sapphire pleases herself where she works, and doesn't take on long commitments—and we all know why, don't we?' she tacked on meaningly. 'A certain person might want her to sing at a special party.'

Thea had looked at Pauline. 'Marcus Conan, you mean?' she had asked, although she knew the answer.

Pauline had nodded knowingly. 'Of course,' she said. 'He's her open sesame to all the hotel bookings she gets. She has no worry about looking for work, not when she has friends like that. If that's what you can call it,' she tacked on meaningly.

After this, Thea had quickly changed the conver-

sation. She could see that Pauline was settling down
to a good gossip, and was sure to mention Marcus's
fiancée some time during the conversation, and the
less said about that the better, from Thea's point of
view.

The stark fact that Sapphire's future was assured
by her connection with Marcus echoed her own
unhappy experience. Thea would not have got the
job she now held if it had not been for him, she was
absolutely certain.

It was not as if she had wanted his help, she
thought bleakly, but she had got it all the same, and
that placed her in the same category as Sapphire,
just one of the women in his life. Even though the
help he had given her was not given for the same
reasons that he had helped Sapphire with her career
it still made her feel like an unwanted dependant,
and hurt her pride.

Now that she had had time to reassemble her
thoughts on the surprising appearance of Marcus
that night, she had undergone a change of opinion.
The excuse she had brought forward earlier, that he
could not have known that she was on duty, no
longer held credence. He must have known why
Sapphire was there, and had probably arranged the
whole thing.

This conclusion had brought her to another and
even less palatable conclusion, and that was that
there had been a purpose behind his action. What
that purpose was, Thea couldn't even hazard a
guess, and it annoyed her. It could have been his
way of keeping tabs on her, but this seemed a ridiculous way of going about it. He could have done
that without too much trouble, she thought; she was

employed in a hotel that was under his managerial control, and there was certainly no need to foist Sapphire on her. He could not have been blind to the animosity Sapphire held towards her.

It could also have been an egotistical action on his part. Under that smooth exterior of his, was he absolutely furious with her for breaking off the engagement? she wondered. Michael hadn't been the only one who had said that he was hard. Pauline had hinted as much as well, she recalled. In which case, the sooner she got out the better, Thea told herself, although she could hardly believe that a man of Marcus's stamp would stoop to such petty retaliation. On the other hand, he must have known that Sapphire's presence in the hotel would make life difficult for her. She took a deep sigh. Nothing was adding up.

At the thought of explaining to Pauline why she wanted to change her job, so soon after she had started there, Thea almost changed her mind, and wondered if she could possibly hang on until Sapphire's three-month run was over, but the thought of seeing Marcus collect her from the hotel each evening, for she was bound to have to do another late afternoon duty during that period, gave her the courage to go ahead. She was still in love with him, no matter what type of man he was, and she had been hurt enough without having to suffer the torment of seeing him with someone else. Only by removing herself right out of his vicinity could she hope to survive and make another life for herself.

On the Friday morning before Sapphire was due to sing on the Saturday, she made an impromptu visit to the hotel, and seeing her, Thea steeled her-

self to meet Marcus again. She had not envisaged
Sapphire paying a morning visit, and even Pauline
was surprised to see her.

'Tell Mr Bois that I'd like a look at the stage posi-
tioning,' she commanded Thea.

'I'm afraid my uncle's out at the moment,' Pauline got in quickly. 'The stage is being erected at the
end of the dining room. I can show you where, but
it won't be put up until tomorrow night.'

Sapphire stared at Pauline as if she was an interesting specimen she had just chanced upon. 'Dining
room?' she echoed haughtily, then gave an elegant
shrug of her slim shoulders. 'Oh well, if that's the
best you can do.' She then thought for a moment. 'I
shall not, I hope, be competing with the soup
course, or the main course come to that. I trust
arrangements have been made in that direction?'
she demanded of Pauline.

'Of course,' replied an equally annoyed Pauline,
who would obviously have loved to verify her fears.
'Would you like to see the dining room?' she added,
trying not to let her temper get the better of her.

'There's hardly any point, is there?' Sapphire replied insolently, then turned back to Thea, completely ignoring Pauline. 'Ring for a taxi for me,
will you? and then ring Mr Conan and tell him that
I got through earlier than expected, and that I'll
meet him for lunch at the usual place.'

Pauline's gasp of indignation was quite audible,
but Sapphire ignored it and walked over to the same
lounge seat that she had sat in the night Marcus had
collected her, leaving Thea the embarrassment of
ringing Marcus after she had made the call to the
taxi number.

It was too much to hope for that Marcus would not be in his office; he was, of course, and Thea, pretending that she did not recognise his voice, gave the bare message as it had been given her, and called him Mr Conan.

His amused, 'Thank you, Thea,' made her slam the receiver down harder than was absolutely necessary, but she did not intend to indulge in a conversation with him, not with the silent but very observant Sapphire listening in.

When Sapphire had left, Pauline gave vent to her exasperation. 'Of all the objectionable females!' she exclaimed indignantly. 'Imagine having her around for three whole months! I'm not sure I'm going to be able to take it,' she wailed.

'I feel exactly the same way,' Thea endorsed heartily. 'You wouldn't know of any other hotel that requires a well-trained receptionist, would you? One that definitely does not go in for entertaining the guests?'

Pauline gave an appreciative grin. 'Two well-trained receptionists,' she commented, but when her smile was not echoed by Thea she gave her a searching look. 'You really meant that, didn't you?' she asked in a surprised way.

Thea gave her an apologetic smile and nodded. 'I've been seriously considering moving on for several days now.'

'Jobs aren't all that easy to come by,' Pauline replied. 'And I shouldn't worry about her, you won't be seeing all that much of her, you know.' Her glance strayed to the poster depicting Sapphire's photograph. 'Let's hope she's a flop,' she said grimly. 'I think she'd go down very well with the

gurgling of the soup course,' she added maliciously,
then gave Thea another wide grin. 'Come on, don't
let the likes of her get you down. Do what I do, grit
your teeth and bear it!'

Thea looked away from Pauline's amused eyes.
Where did she go from there? How could she possibly explain the reason why she had to go without
telling her the truth? In the end she settled for an
airy approach to the matter by saying, 'I guess I've
got the wanderlust. I used to be a dental nurse. Oh,
I like this work,' she added quickly, seeing Pauline's
eyebrows raise, 'but I'm not sure that I'd want to
settle for it permanently. I really haven't had a
chance to explore the possibilities of going back to
my previous work.'

Pauline was silent for a second or so while she
studied Thea with her head on one side and a
puzzled look in her eyes. 'Why did you come out
here? To stay, I mean?' she asked Thea bluntly.
'You don't seem to be the wanderlust type to me.'
This time it was Thea who raised her brows. 'We've
had them here from time to time, English,
American, French—they ask for work, but you
know they'll never settle. Give them a month or so,
and they're off again. Going to see the world, they
say.' Pauline stared down at the desk top. 'Hopeless
romantics, that's what they are,' she added. 'Always
looking for something. The girls for romance—the
men——' she gave a light shrug, 'adventure, I suppose—whatever it is, I don't believe they'd recognise it when they saw it.'

Her gaze then left the desk top and settled on the
windows to the view beyond, and following her gaze
Thea saw the white plumes of spray as the waves

caressed the shore of the bay in the far distance. 'I'm sure all that moving around is bound to have an effect on them,' she went on. 'I remember one girl,' she told Thea thoughtfully, 'she told me she wanted to see as much of the world as she could before she settled down under a line of diapers.' Her expression lightened as she said this and she smiled. 'You should have seen her, she would have looked more at home under the movie lights! She had gorgeous red hair, tinted, I suspect, and painted nails to match. She always looked as if she had just stepped out of a beauty salon. I had a hard time imagining her under a line of diapers, I can tell you!' Her mood changed to a serious one. 'As I said, you're not one of them, so what are you doing so far from home?'

Thea's grey eyes met Pauline's brown searching eyes. 'I came because of my brother. He got a job out here, and sent for me when he decided to settle here,' she replied quietly.

Pauline's eyes widened in interest. 'Where's he working?' she asked.

Thea's eyes clouded over; but she would have to get used to this poignant questioning. 'He died in a car crash the day before I arrived,' she said in a low voice.

'Gee, honey, I'm sorry,' Pauline said quickly, then gave a small gasp. 'I remember reading about it! Michael someone——' she half muttered to herself. 'He was an architect, wasn't he, and was doing some work for Mr Conan?'

Thea looked away quickly. It would only be a matter of minutes now before Pauline got the connection between her and Marcus, and she ought to have thought of that.

As if right on cue, Pauline's eyes went wide. 'But it was his sister who was engaged to Mr Conan,' she gasped, and stared hard at Thea.

Thea couldn't meet Pauline's eyes and stared out of the window. She couldn't have hoped to go on deceiving her, not on an island of this size, and particularly with anything that concerned such an august personage as Marcus Conan. 'That's right,' she said quietly.

Pauline shook her head disbelievingly. 'I don't get this,' she said slowly. 'If you're engaged to Marcus Conan, what are you doing here?'

Thea studied the gentle surge of the waves in the distance. 'I was engaged to Marcus, I'm not now. I needed a job, so here I am,' she supplied indifferently.

Pauline drew in a deep breath as she sat down slowly on a chair. 'You mean he asked you to marry him, and then broke it off?' she demanded.

Thea gave a thin smile. 'I broke it off, to be more precise,' she replied. 'I could see it wasn't going to work out, so I—please, Pauline, it's very personal, and I'd really rather not talk about it,' she added softly.

'You can't leave me in the air like that!' Pauline squeaked. 'You get engaged to the most eligible bachelor on the island, not only eligible, but disgustingly rich, and handsome to boot, and you just stand there and tell me that you broke it off——' she shook her head in a dazed way. 'This is screwy,' she muttered.

Thea eyed the bemused Pauline. 'Can you honestly see a man like that settling for someone like me?' she asked sardonically. 'He only asked me to marry him because he felt responsible for me. There was nothing else in it.' Her eyes clouded over as she looked away from Pauline's searching eyes. 'Oh, yes, for a while I lived on cloud seven, thinking how marvellous things would be, but you can't live on dreams, it's much better to face reality,' she added on a bitter note.

An influx of newcomers cut short whatever Pauline had wanted to say to this bald comment of Thea's, and the girls were kept busy until their lunch break, which they took in the hotel's dining room in a sectioned-off area near the kitchen entrance.

Any hope that Pauline might drop the subject was quickly dispelled by her opening words as soon as they had been served with their salad. 'He must have felt something for you, Thea,' she said, as though there had been no break in their conversation. 'I mean—well, marriage isn't a thing you take on lightly. Besides,' she grinned, 'you can have too much of a good thing, you know. Men nearly always settle for the homely types, easier to live with, if you know what I mean.'

'Thank you,' Thea replied, unable to suppress a smile at Pauline at the way she had labelled her as the homely type.

'Oh, you know what I mean!' Pauline added with a chuckle. 'And stop selling yourself short. You've a lot more going for you than that Sapphire has. Given a year or so, she'll start to look hagridden, she gets her face out of a box. All right, I'm a cat,' she grinned, 'but her sort gets me on the raw. So she has a good figure—well, so have you, a bit on the thin side, maybe, but just right for your height. I'd back you against her, any day.'

There was silence while the girls ate their lunch,
but their thoughts were far away from their cheese
salad. 'What did he say when you broke it off?'
Pauline asked curiously, as she pushed her empty
plate away.

Thea put down her knife and fork. She hadn't
finished her salad, but she had had enough. 'Nothing,' she replied quietly, 'just accepted it, and
proved that I was right, and that he was only out to
protect my future.'

Pauline gave her a sympathetic smile. 'Well,
never mind, pet. There's plenty of fish in the sea. I'd
say you did right in breaking it off. He wouldn't
have allowed you to back out of the engagement if
he'd really cared for you, not if what I've heard
about him is right. He's a hard man to cross. He's
respected and feared by a great many folk, but he's
a just man for all that, it's the shady dealers who
have cause to fear him.'

The girls refused dessert and settled for coffee,
and after a few minutes' silence Pauline said rum-
natively, 'What rotten luck that she'd come across
you. If Uncle hadn't had that good idea she'd never
have seen you.'

Thea's thoughts did not coincide with Pauline's,
for unless she was very much mistaken it had not
been her uncle's idea at all, but one that had been
put to him by one of his bosses—but she could not be
absolutely certain of this, she thought absently, as she
refused a second cup of coffee. 'Does he often get
these sort of ideas, about livening up the guests' stay?'
she asked idly.

Pauline gave an airy wave of the hand. 'Well, I

know he's my uncle,' she said, 'but the sad fact is he hasn't an original thought in his head. He's all for a quiet life. I suppose one of the guests must have asked if the hotel ever put on any entertainment. I can't see him bothering otherwise.'

'Or the idea was put to him by one of the directors,' said Thea, speaking her thoughts out loud without giving herself time to think.

'Marcus Conan, for instance?' Pauline replied, quickly catching on to Thea's line of reasoning and somewhat shaking Thea with her perspicacity.

'Oh, I wasn't really thinking of him,' Thea lied, but it was too late now, for Pauline had got the bit between her teeth.

'It could very well have been him,' Pauline commented thoughtfully. 'Our Sapphire could have got bored with her usual haunts and asked him to come up with something.' She stared at Thea. 'If it was him, then it was pretty foul of him to suggest this place, wasn't it? I mean, he knew you were here, didn't he? He must have got you the job, but that's men all over,' she said exasperatedly, 'it wouldn't occur to him that Sapphire would have it in for you.'

Thea chose to ignore the last comment; her thoughts were on Pauline's previous statement. 'Are you sure that Marcus got me the job?' she asked in a deceptively mild voice.

Pauline nodded emphatically. 'I wasn't before, but I am now,' she said. 'I told you my uncle isn't one to stick his neck out. We've had so many of the travelling fraternity and the constant stops and starts that it's now the rule of the house not to employ what we term as "strays". They have to be

locals now. You were the exception to the rule, and
it's pretty obvious now why you were taken on.'

Thea felt a surge of hopelessness wash over her.
'Do all the other hotels have the same rule?' she
asked Pauline quietly.

Pauline blinked at the change of conversation.
'Why, I expect so,' she said slowly. 'I don't honestly
know, though.'

Thea's forefinger traced the rim of her coffee cup.
'In that case, it looks as if I shall have to stay put.
I've no option,' she said dully.

'Come on, cheer up,' Pauline said heartily, as she
poured herself a third cup of coffee. 'Although I
don't think I'd care to be in your position,' she
admitted honestly, 'not with someone like that on
the warpath.' She was silent as she sipped her
coffee, then said thoughtfully, 'It's no wonder she's
gunning for you.'

There was no need to ask who Pauline was referring to, and Thea gave a light shrug. 'It doesn't
make sense, really,' she said after a moment's
thought. 'I'm out of the running, and she's back in
favour. You'd think she'd leave it at that, wouldn't
you?'

Pauline gave her a knowing look. 'Not Sapphire
Durley,' she said emphatically. 'You're still around,
and that's enough for her. I can see your point in
wanting to remove yourself from the limelight,
though, and under the circumstances I might be
able to help you out there.'

Thea's eyes showed their appreciation of this offer
of Pauline's. 'I don't mind what I do,' she said
quickly. 'It need only be something to tide me over
until I get myself properly settled,' she added.

Pauline's eyes were narrowed in thought. 'I'm thinking that perhaps an aunt of mine could do with some help. She runs a small guesthouse and beach café, and she's not so young as she was. It's nothing grand, mind you, but she's got room to put you up as well,' she said.

'Oh, Pauline!' breathed Thea thankfully. 'Do you really think she'd take me on? But what about your uncle? Won't he be furious at my leaving so soon?' she queried anxiously.

'Don't worry about that,' Pauline said confidently. 'I'd just say that you've been offered a job more in keeping with your past training, he won't argue about it, especially as you-know-who recommended you for the job in the first place. Uncle Joseph is all for a quiet life, as I told you. Leave it to me. I'll see what I can fix up for you.'

Thea could have hugged Pauline, for she was sure that she would get her the job that she had mentioned, and with any luck she would be well away from Sapphire and Marcus's vicinity before many days had passed.

It was as well for Thea's peace of mind that she had the promise of Pauline's help in removing her from the hotel, for Sapphire's appearance the following evening brought another round of ammunition directed at her by the barely civil singer, who had swept into the hotel in a towering rage ten minutes before she was due to give a performance.

'Have there been any messages for me?' she demanded of Thea haughtily.

Thea had looked at Pauline, who had given a negative shake of the head. 'No message,' Thea had replied, her blunt answer echoing Sapphire's bald approach. She knew her name, Thea thought, but she had addressed her as if she were a servant.

Sapphire's lips had thinned at Thea's response. 'Well, there will be,' she said softly. 'Just make sure that it's passed on to me.' Her flashing eyes left Thea and rested on the lobby door. 'Something must have held him up,' she said, her tapping foot displaying her displeasure, then she looked directly at Thea. 'But no doubt he'll make up for it,' she commented meaningly, with a small hard smile at her, then swept towards the dining room and her awaiting audience.

Pauline's look was eloquent as her eyes followed Sapphire's tall figure as it disappeared through the glass doors leading to the dining room. 'And we love you too,' she said gratingly, and looked at Thea. 'I think he wants his head examined,' she commented acidly, then gave a sigh. 'Still, there's no accounting for tastes, is there?'

Thea managed a weak smile and looked hopefully towards the lobby clock. With any luck she would be off duty before Marcus put in an appearance, since it was obvious that Sapphire expected him to attend her first night.

Thea's luck held and she went off duty with much more studious attention to the 'time up' slogan than she might otherwise have done, and fairly raced for the seclusion of her room.

The following morning a pleased Pauline told her that Sapphire's anticipation of either hearing from Marcus or having him attend her performance had not been fulfilled. He had neither rung nor put in an appearance. 'She tore into the night clerk,' she commented, 'insisted that there must have been a message left for her, and hinted darkly that the previous receptionist must have taken the call and failed to pass it on to him.' She gave a grimace. 'She was trying to make trouble for you, obviously—she wouldn't bother about me. They had to ring for a taxi for her, and she was spitting mad about it, she'd relied on another form of transport apparently, and you know what it's like getting a taxi at that time of night,' she grinned. 'Serves her right for being so beastly to you, and I hope he was entertaining someone else!'

Thea looked away quickly so that Pauline would not see the hurt these words had caused her. It was bad enough knowing that Marcus was with Sapphire, but to bring another beauty into his life was too much for her to take.

'We're going to see my aunt this morning,' Pauline announced, as she helped Thea to make her bed. 'I was going to leave it until next week, I usually visit once a week, but I've a feeling that the sooner that I get you out of here, the better.'

Her words echoed Thea's own thoughts on the matter, and she gave her a grateful smile. 'Let's hope she takes to me,' she commented quietly.

Pauline's aunt, Mrs Welling, was a widow in her early seventies, and Thea took to her on sight and fervently hoped that the feeling was mutual. Her iron-grey hair was plaited and arranged in a bun at the back of her head, and her thin slightly stooped figure gave evidence of a hardworking life, as did her work-roughened hands.

When Pauline explained the reason for her mission, saying breezily after she had introduced Thea, 'Thea's looking for a job, Aunt, and I wondered if you could do with any help.'

Mrs Welling's lively brown eyes had passed over
Thea, and although the look had been a swift one,
Thea felt that she had missed nothing, and wished
she had worn her cotton blouse and jeans rather
than the dress she had chosen, for its pink and white
striped bodice and flared skirt was more in keeping
with a sedate coffee morning gathering than an ap-
plication for work.

'I'm not denying that I could use some help,' she
admitted slowly. 'I'm fully booked at this time of
year, and the café is taking up more of my time
these days.' She gave Thea a hard searching stare.
'It's hard work, though,' and she looked pointedly
at Thea's soft white hands.

'I don't mind what I do,' Thea got in quickly,
seeing herself losing this opportunity of removing
herself from the hotel.

'There's crates of soft drinks,' Mrs Welling went
on firmly, refusing to let this nice but rather slightly
built girl, who didn't look as if she belonged this end
of town at all, persuade her to make a mistake. She
didn't want to have to apologise for the menial tasks
she would have to ask her to do. 'And they have to
be humped from the road to the café, and trays of
hamburgers to be carted from the house to the
beach,' she went on, fixing a bright stare at Thea, as
if daring her to take the work on.

'I'm sure I'll be able to manage,' Thea said
hastily. 'I'm quite strong,' she added lamely, not
knowing what else she could say to persuade Mrs
Welling to take her on.

'Why not have a trial period?' Pauline suggested
helpfully. 'Give it, say, a fortnight. By then you'll

both know if the work's too heavy for Thea,' and she looked hopefully at her aunt.

Mrs Welling considered this for a moment or so, then nodded her head. 'Very well,' she said slowly, and looked at Thea. 'I'll say what I think, mind you. If I feel that you're not up to the work, I shall say so,' she warned Thea, who was certain she could manage all that would be required of her.

Now that that was settled, Mrs Welling proceeded to outline the kind of work Thea would have to cope with, while Pauline made herself busy making them some coffee.

'The café's on the beach,' Mrs Welling began. 'It's not strictly what you would term a café, I don't cater for hot meals or hot drinks—just soft drinks, cookies and hamburgers, but we do a good trade all the year round. Andy was kept pretty busy, wasn't he, Pauline?' she asked, as Pauline brought in the coffee tray, and Pauline nodded in confirmation.

'That's why I brought Thea here,' said Pauline as she laid out the cups and saucers. 'I didn't see how you were going to manage now that he's taken that job on John's ship.'

Mrs Welling's brown eyes rested fondly on her niece, and she gave a slight sigh. 'If I'd been younger I'd have been able to cope. I suppose you're right, though.' She turned her attention back to Thea again. 'I've six boarders, you see, and they're regulars, no trouble at all. Out all day, and I fix them an evening meal, they've steady jobs in the town and have been with me for years. I don't cater for the tourists as far as accommodation is concerned, and the café isn't opened until midday, and that's when we do most of our trade. We don't stay

open late either, most of the tourists have had
enough by about six, and wander back to their
hotels to get ready for their evening meals.' She gave
another long sigh. 'As I was saying, once I could
cope——'

'But you can't now,' Pauline broke in swiftly, as
she handed her aunt her coffee, 'so you'll just have
to give in. Thea will be able to help with the filling
of the hamburgers—oh, and lots of things. Andy
helped with the café, of course, but there wasn't
much else he could do in the house, was there?' she
said coaxingly. 'I'm sure you'll find Thea's a
treasure, and she can have Andy's room, can't she?'
she added persuasively.

Her aunt gave her a suspicious look. 'Got it all
worked out, have you?' she demanded, then her face
relaxed into a smile as her eyes met Pauline's laugh-
ing ones. 'Well, we'll see,' she conceded.

CHAPTER FOUR

ONE week later Thea started work for Pauline's aunt. She had moved in on the previous Saturday morning, thus avoiding another encounter with Sapphire.

As Pauline had predicted, Thea had met with no opposition from Mr Bois when she had told him she was leaving, explaining somewhat apologetically that she had found a job more suited to her capabilities, and this had been received with understanding resignation from the manager in a manner that suggested that he had foreseen such an event, and proved conclusively to Thea that Marcus had been instrumental in getting her the job.

Beach House was an old, rather ramshackle building, that had once been white and was now badly in need of a coat of paint. As its name suggested, it was built on a slight incline directly opposite the beach, and the café that Mrs Welling had mentioned was only a few yards from the house and situated directly on the beach. Although called a café, it was more in the nature of a kiosk with a counter for serving and for leaning on, as no chairs were provided, and would not have been used if they had been, for the refreshments were carried back to the loungers the sunbathers had brought with them for their morning laze in the sun.

After Mrs Welling's rather gloomy prediction of the physical strength required for such work and her

doubts that Thea would be able to manage, Thea
had been determined to somehow cope with the
challenge, the greatest of which would be the carrying of the crates of soft drinks from the house to the
café. It was just a case of getting used to the weight,
she told herself. After all, Mrs Welling had managed
it for years, and she and Thea were much of the
same height and slim build, and if she could do it, so
could Thea.

Thea had no other worry about the work, and as
the drinks were only delivered once a week, she
reasoned that she ought to have recovered from
whatever physical exhaustion she suffered from the
task by the time the next delivery was due.

Although Thea had enjoyed working at the hotel,
until Sapphire's arrival, that was, she found this
work much more to her liking. With only six
boarders in the house, who mainly looked after the
general tidying of their rooms, which were given a
vacuum and polish once a week, the work in the
house was no hardship, since everything ran like
clockwork, and Thea would find herself begging
Mrs Welling to let her do certain jobs around the
house in the mornings, for her afternoons were spent
at the beach café and were more like a holiday than
actual work.

After three days she had managed to take over
some of the work, in spite of Mrs Welling's grum-
bling complaint that she wasn't ready for the rock-
ing chair yet, a remark which Thea took with a grin
and otherwise ignored, for it was plain that Mrs
Welling was extremely grateful for the help and
treated Thea more as a niece of hers than an em-
ployee, and a strong friendship had already grown

up between them.

When the consignment of soft drinks arrived on the Wednesday, Mrs Welling had given Thea a worried look and then looked back at the pile of boxes and several wooden crates piled up outside the house. 'That's as far as the lorry can come,' she said. 'They get bogged down in the sand if they go any further.'

'It's all right,' Thea had assured her quickly, with more confidence than she had felt, for there did seem an awful lot of cartons there. At least they were cartons, she thought stoutly, and not many wooden crates. 'I haven't far to carry them, have I?' she added, and met the old lady's eyes firmly. 'And I know about the doctor's orders, so don't you dare try to give me a hand,' she said firmly.

'I ought to hire a boy for the rough work,' Mrs Welling said, and took a deep breath. 'That's what we'll do.'

'We'll do no such thing,' Thea replied hastily. 'Who's going to take on work that only comes once a week?' she pointed out. 'What would they do the rest of the time? You promised to let me try, didn't you?' she said coaxingly. 'I'll do the rolls and hamburgers first, then I'll start on the cases. I should be finished in time to open at midday,' she went on determinedly, not allowing the old lady to contradict her, for she also knew that Mrs Welling couldn't afford to get any extra help; Pauline had put her in the picture there. Most of her savings had gone to help her nephew Andy get a good education, and she had not sought a high rent from her boarders, who although they held steady jobs, were not in the high wage bracket, and were more in the nature of old friends whom she wouldn't dream of embarrassing by demanding the going rate for boarding. In return for her kindness, any wage raise that they received was automatically passed on to her, but these were few and far between.

The wage that Thea had accepted had been a very moderate one, and Mrs Welling had known it, since she was not ignorant of the high wages that could be earned in the tourist boom on the island, but as Thea had said, she had her board taken care of, and her meals, and if one took all that into consideration, she was really getting a very good salary, plus, she had jokingly added, all the sun and fresh air she could wish for, and she wasn't sure that she oughtn't to be paying Mrs Welling for the privilege of working in such pleasant surroundings!

Thea had spoken the truth here, for she was ideally suited. She loved the kiosk work that had already turned her pale skin a honey shade, and soon she would be as tanned as the locals. The holiday atmosphere was invigorating too, everybody was pleasant and very helpful, and it wasn't like work at all. There was one other great advantage too, the absence of the island's wealthier inhabitants. The more luxurious hotel complexes had their own private beaches where refreshments were brought to them by waiters from the hotel, and who would have considered this small golden beach somewhat lacking in amenities. The beach was used mainly by tourists who had booked into one of the numerous hotels in Charlotte Amalie and who required no other facilities apart from sunshine and a space in which to acquire a tan.

When Thea had finished preparing the rolls and

hamburgers, she carried the trays down to the kiosk, then started on the carrying of the drinks.

'Those cases are heavier than they look,' Mrs Welling warned her as she began to pick up the first one, then taking a deep breath she disappeared back into the house as if unable to bear to watch the rest of the proceedings.

By the time Thea had carried the first six cases the hundred-yard distance to the kiosk, she could well verify Mrs Welling's comments as to their weight, for they were filled with cartons of orange juice, and each case felt that much heavier than the previous one, and there were only, she thought dismally, one dozen more to go, plus three crates of bottled minerals.

It was sheer determination that kept her going, telling herself that once she was used to the work, she wouldn't feel the terrible ache in her arms that she was now feeling, and the thought that Mrs Welling had managed to cope all those years was an added spur.

She had just placed the seventh container by the kiosk, and stopped to get her breath before returning for another, when a very familiar voice cut across her tired senses. 'What the devil are you doing?'

Thea straightened her aching back before turning to meet Marcus's furious eyes. 'I'm working,' she said simply, turning to catch a case that was about to fall from the precarious position she had plumped it down in in her anxiety to relieve herself of the load.

Marcus looked from her to the remaining cases back at the house, and without a word grimly marched over to them and ignoring Thea's weak

protest of, 'I can manage,' completed the cartage in
a remarkably short time, then proceeded to load the
cases into the kiosk with an indignant Thea standing
helplessly by.

'So this is where you've hidden yourself, is it?' he
said grimly, fastidiously dusting a few grains of sand
off his smartly cut navy blue blazer. 'What was
wrong with the hotel work?' he demanded.

Thea's furious eyes met Marcus's equally furious
ones. 'Nothing was wrong with it,' she replied
crossly. 'I just felt in need of a change. There's a
nothing wrong with that, is there?' she challenged
him, as if he didn't know why she had left, she
thought furiously. Pauline had said that such a
thought wouldn't occur to him, but Thea knew different. Sapphire had had it in for her right from the
start of their acquaintance, and Marcus was not that
blind.

'It didn't occur to you that you might have con-
sulted me first, I suppose?' Marcus grated, and Thea
could see that he was absolutely furious with her
and it occurred to her that he might not think the
job she had taken suitable for an ex-fiancée of his—
and that was just too bad, she thought acidly.

'As a matter of fact, it did,' she replied calmly,
'but I didn't see why I should bother you. I'm perfectly happy,' she added firmly. 'Mrs Welling's a
darling, and I love the work.'

Marcus's eyes went from her brightly flushed
cheeks to a streak of dust across her smooth forehead
where she had brushed a tired hand during her
earlier excursions. 'You're not going to be much use
to her with a strained back,' he commented bitingly.
'It's time she handed this part of the work over to a

man—or employed a boy to do the rough work. I'm not having you breaking your back on it, that's for sure,' he said adamantly, and caught one of Thea's hands in his and turning the palm towards him studied the red chafed area in the centre of her palm, and his jaw hardened. 'You're not doing any more rough work,' he shot out at her. 'I'll arrange to have a lad sent down to handle this side of the work.'

Thea's heart was thumping against her ribs as she pulled her hand away from him. His touch could so easily melt any opposition of hers to his wishes, but she meant nothing to him, it was only his personal pride that had made him seek her out. 'Don't you dare send anyone down here to help out, I'll lose my job if you do, Mrs Welling can't afford to employ two helpers.'

'I'm not asking her to,' Marcus replied haughtily. 'The lad works for me.'

'But you can't do that!' Thea gasped. 'What am I to say to her? No! I'm sorry, I can't accept any help.'

Marcus's green eyes narrowed to a slit. 'Then go back to the hotel,' he said softly. 'The job's still open.'

Thea stared at him; he was quite serious. 'I'm not going back,' she said quietly, and added flatly, 'Thank you, anyway, for thinking of me.'

Marcus continued to study her, making her bright cheeks turn a deeper hue, and she felt like an obstinate child wilfully refusing to conform over something that was for her benefit—only it wasn't to her benefit, she thought wretchedly. He was acting as if he owned her, and he didn't. He could adopt such an attitude with Sapphire, but not with her. She might

be his ex-fiancée, but that was as far as it went; he
had no other claim on her.

'It wouldn't be because of Sapphire, would it?' he
asked softly.

Thea's eyes spoke volumes, but she answered
calmly enough for all the turmoil going on inside
her. 'Of course not!' she said scornfully. 'She can't
help her nature, but I must admit that I was glad to
get out of her proximity,' she added forcefully.

Marcus's eyes showed his amusement at this, and
Thea wanted to hit out at him. Pauline must have
been right after all, she thought miserably; it hadn't
occurred to him that Sapphire would set out to
make trouble for her.

'Do I detect a spark of green in your eyes?'
Marcus queried in the same soft voice that had a
wealth of meaning behind it.

Thea looked away quickly from those eyes of his
that saw too much for her liking. What a beastly
thing to say! she thought indignantly. Was she jealous of Sapphire? was what he was asking her. A
lump came into her throat as she considered the
question and how she ought to answer it, but she
failed to come up with a suitable reply and thought
it would be safer to ignore it. Why couldn't they
leave her alone? Her wide grey eyes met Marcus's
enigmatic ones. 'Leave me alone, Marcus,' she said
in a low flat voice, then glanced at her watch. 'It's
time I was getting back to the house,' she added.

The amusement had gone from his eyes as he
gave her a long studied look. 'Very well,' he said
abruptly, and turned on his heel. 'You may get back
to your work. As for your other request, I've no intention of giving a promise on something I don't

intend to keep.' The next minute he was striding away from her.

Thea stood watching his tall figure until it passed out of her sight. Her heart was hammering at an alarming rate as she recalled those last telling words of his, and her spirits soared up into the bright blue sky above her as she walked slowly back to the house. Was he telling her that he loved her, she wondered, and if so, why hadn't he said so?

By the time she had reached the house the answer was in front of her, and it was no use trying to delude herself otherwise. Marcus felt responsible for her, and that was the beginning and the end of his interest in her. He would continue to watch over her, was what he had really meant—and, heartsore, Thea had had to admit to this one and only reason for his persistence.

All she could hope for was that in time this interest would surely wane. He was a very busy man and would shortly find the task of keeper to a very uninteresting English girl an irksome one and write her off the books. What she needed, she told herself stoutly, was another interest, preferably male, and someone in a responsible position whom Marcus could trust to look after her interests and thereby letting him off the hook.

But where could such a character be found? she wondered as she slipped into the back of the house and up the stairs to her room before Mrs Welling knew she was back and who would now be fixing their lunch. Someone, she mused, who would be satisfied with her companionship and nothing else, for she had no intention of entering into another emotional void—not that she ever would. Marcus had her heart and would always hold it. There would be no one else for her and no fulfilment of his love, but she could still dream, couldn't she? She didn't even regret the fact that she had ever met him—how could she? He had given her a brief glimpse of happiness that she might never have known, and however hard it was for her now to face reality, she would never forget him.

Her musings were cut short by a short gasp of consternation as she caught sight of herself in the bathroom mirror. No wonder he had made her feel like a wilful child. She looked like one, and a very grubby one at that!

To think that she had once imagined that he loved her, she thought sadly as her eyes traced the long smear of dust across her forehead, and she shook her head at her reflection. Companionship, she told herself, was about all she would get, she would have no worry of anyone going off the deep end with her.

After a quick shower she changed into a halter dress that would give her the maximum amount of the sunshine that would stream into the kiosk and complete her tan, then went to find Mrs Welling.

'Very nice,' commented Mrs Welling, as she put a plate of ham salad in front of her, and gave her a smile. 'I didn't have that kind of help in my day.'

Thea had thought that she was referring to her dress, and her heart sank as she realised that she was referring to Marcus. She might have known that Mrs Welling would have kept a strict eye on her progress, ready to rush out and assist should the going get too hard for Thea. Any minute now she would be asking who he was; it would be a quite

natural question and purely out of interest and not
inquisitiveness, yet Thea was loth to supply the
answer, since it would invariably lead to other questions. 'Oh, I was lucky, wasn't I?' she managed to
reply breezily. 'So I cheated a bit, didn't I? I did get
some training in, though,' she added with a bright
smile. 'We'll see how we get on next week.'

'It was Marcus Conan, wasn't it?' Mrs Welling
commented. 'A fine-looking man, too. I've seen
plenty of photographs of him in the island magazine, he's quite well known. Fancy him stopping to
help you out!'

This was said in an absentminded way, but Thea
was not fooled. The old lady was consumed with
curiosity, but for politeness' sake was determined not
to show it. Thea sighed inwardly. So much for
trying to lose herself in the island's quieter section,
and the last place she thought Marcus would find
her. 'It's not really so odd,' she said carefully. 'He
does know me. My brother used to work for him
—' She stopped abruptly; surely she wouldn't have
to go through all that miserable explanation again?

Mrs Welling gave her a look of sympathy. 'Pauline told me about that. I'm sorry, Thea. It must
have been dreadful for you, coming all that way to
join him, and for that to happen. Now finish your
lunch,' she ordered kindly, 'I mustn't keep you talking or there'll be a queue outside the kiosk waiting
for your arrival.'

Thea got on with her lunch and inwardly blessed
Pauline for her thoughtfulness. It was obvious that
she had kept the news of Thea's engagement to
Marcus from her aunt, and Thea was grateful that it
had been of such a short duration that it had not got

into the island's magazine.

The next few days passed peacefully enough for
Thea, except for the appearance of a tall rangy-
looking islander with ebony black skin and large
ultra-white teeth which flashed in his dark shad-
owed features with amazing regularity whenever
Thea's puzzled eyes rested on him, and it wasn't
until she tried to carry out a few empty returnable
crates ready to take them back to the house for col-
lection the following Wednesday, when the next delivery was due, that she realised why he was there,
and no number of protests that she could manage
the crates, they were empty after all, would serve to
put him off his task. He just gave her a wide grin
and carried on as if she hadn't spoken.

Sam Jacks, as she discovered his name was, was
there the following day, and the day after that, and
Thea began to feel crossly as if she was under house
arrest. There was absolutely no reason why poor
Sam should have to while his day away on the off-
chance that there would be some carrying for him to
do. It was absolutely ridiculous, she fumed, after
putting up with it for three days. She would ring
Marcus and order him to call off his watchdog. If he
insisted on her not doing any carrying of the heavy
cases, then he could get Sam to make an appearance
on the day the deliveries were expected, and that
was as far as she would allow him to help out! It
wasn't going to be easy explaining Sam's presence to
Mrs Welling, who was bound to worry about giving
him some compensation for his work, and that
would not do at all.

When Mrs Welling was busy dusting the guests'
bedrooms the following morning, Thea took the

opportunity of ringing Marcus and demanding that he find other work for his 'lad'. She ought to remember to thank him as well, she told herself while she waited for the call to be answered. She didn't want to sound ungrateful, but enough was enough!

To her vexation, Marcus wasn't available, and she had to leave a message with his secretary. Thea gave her name, and left a message to the effect that she wished to thank Mr Conan for his help, but the vacancy had now been filled, and he could release Mr Jacks from his duties.

That, she told herself as she put the telephone down, was that—and, she hoped, the end of any other interference from Marcus.

That evening, however, Thea was to learn that once Marcus's mind was set on a course no persuasion would alter it. Thea was also beginning to see the other side of the man she had nearly married, the side that Michael had seen and Pauline had mentioned. An implacable side of a man who was master of his ship and woe betide anyone who disputed this fact.

When Thea returned to the house after giving Sam a polite 'goodnight' and thinking that she would miss his cheerful company the next day, she found Mrs Welling waiting for her in the hall, and judging by the flustered expression on her face, Thea knew that she was concerned about something. 'You aren't thinking of leaving me, are you, Thea?' she asked almost as soon as Thea had closed the door behind her.

Thea's brows lifted in surprise at this unexpected question. 'Of course not,' she replied quickly. 'What makes you ask that?' she queried lightly.

'Well, there was a rather odd telephone message left for you,' Mrs Welling replied slowly. 'I couldn't understand it all, then I thought that perhaps you'd decided the work here didn't suit you and you'd applied elsewhere.'

Thea handed her the bag of takings from the kiosk, and gave her a smile. 'Now why should I do a thing like that?' she demanded. 'You'd better give me the message and we'll try to make some sense of it,' she added soothingly.

Mrs Welling looked relieved by Thea's assurance, then gave a groan of concentration. 'Well, it was from Pirates' Cove,' she said, 'that's that swanky place the other side of town, and they said that I was to thank you for your message and that it was receiving attention, and that they were sending you a list of vacancies,' she ended flatly, giving Thea a long searching look.

Thea's brows went even higher at this. 'Sending me a list of vacancies?' she repeated perplexedly. 'How very odd! I wonder if they've got me mixed up with someone else,' she mused. 'I did ring and leave a message there for Mr Conan,' and catching Mrs Welling's half-accusing expression she added hastily, 'only to thank him, you know, for helping out,' she tacked on lamely, 'but I certainly didn't ask for a job there.'

Mrs Welling's thin gnarled old hands worried the top of the bag Thea had given her, and she looked quickly away from Thea as she said sadly, 'Well, I wouldn't blame you, Thea, if you had. They can afford to pay the highest rates, and they're never short of staff. You wouldn't have any problem, though, getting a job there—I mean, knowing the boss,' she added significantly.

That at least was true, Thea thought as she re-called Marcus's ultimatum of getting help for the rough work or getting another job that did not demand such physical exertion. Then she took a swift inward breath as the message suddenly became clear to her. There had been no mistake, the mes-sage was meant for her and was a clear but ex-tremely annoying reply from Marcus to her request that he remove Sam from his watchdog duty. In other words, he had no intention of doing any such thing until she either went back to the receptionist work at the hotel, or took a similar job at Pirates' Cove. She intended to do neither, she thought furi-ously. Of all the interfering, autocratic—her expres-sion was so fierce that poor Mrs Welling took a step back in surprise and said, 'Thea?'

Thea's grim countenance softened as her eyes rested on the old lady. She would have to explain the reason for her annoyance, she knew. It wouldn't be fair not to. It looked as if Sam Jacks would be around for a long time indeed, and sooner or later Thea would have to put Mrs Welling into the pic-ture. She frowned as she sought the right way to go about it without giving too much away about her past association with Marcus.

If only he would let well alone, she thought with a sigh before she said slowly, 'I'm afraid this is Mr Conan's doing. I told you that I knew him through my brother. Well,' she went on carefully, 'he didn't like to see me doing the humping of those cases, and he suggested that I take lighter work, that's the reason why a list of vacancies is being sent me,' she added quickly, 'although I made it quite clear that I had no intention of seeking other employment—and I haven't,' she repeated earnestly to Mrs Welling. 'I'm perfectly suited. I should hate to go back to hotel desk work, not after all the sunshine I've been able to get serving in the kiosk, not to mention the fresh air,' she added firmly. 'As for the carrying business, I don't have to worry about that part of it now.' She took a deep breath. 'Mr Conan's sent a lad down to help me. I told him not to bother, but he wouldn't listen.'

'That's very kind of him,' Mrs Welling said quickly before Thea could go on. 'I did say we ought to have a lad, didn't I? Mr Conan's perfectly right. Send him up to see me tomorrow, Thea, and I'll put him on the books.'

'You'll do no such thing!' Thea said crossly. 'We don't need any help, and I said as much! If he refuses to listen to me, then that's his responsibility, it's nothing to do with us,' she added adamantly.

'I don't accept that,' Mrs Welling retorted, equally adamant. 'I can't have him working for nothing—you'll do as I say, and no arguing,' she told Thea firmly.

Thea gave a long sigh. 'I knew you'd take it like that,' she said. 'I wouldn't have told you about it. I'd hoped that Mr Conan would listen to reason and leave me to manage my own affairs. That's really the reason why I rang him,' she admitted quietly. 'I hoped to persuade him to remove the help before Wednesday, and you wouldn't have found out about it. I can assure you that Sam is not working for nothing. He's one of Mr Conan's employees, and you're not to offer to pay him anything. He wouldn't accept it if you did, take my word for it.'

Thea could see that Mrs Welling was not at all convinced, and tried again. 'Look,' she said quickly. 'Let me try and explain how it is. I told you my brother worked for Mr Conan, didn't I? Well, it was Mr Conan who met me at the airport and gave me the news of my brother's death,' she hesitated here, and then went on slowly, 'In a way, he feels responsible for me—sorry for me, if you like,' she added, 'and has taken on the job of looking out for me. Now do you understand?' she asked her softly. 'I didn't want it that way, but there's not much that I can do about it, is there? But I will not have him dictating what sort of job I must have. I'm happy here, I told you that, but if you insist on paying Sam Jacks then I shall have to leave. You can't afford to pay both of us, and there's only enough work for one. I know that, and so do you, so be a dear and do what I'm going to do, accept the help we're being given. With any luck Sam will ask to be relieved of his duty—it must be boring for him just hanging around at the kiosk all afternoon,' she ended with a smile.

Mrs Welling's expression lightened, but there was still doubt in her eyes as she said slowly, 'Well, if you're sure . . .'

'I'm sure,' Thea repeated firmly. 'Now, how about some tea, then I'll help you get dinner.'

A little later Thea started to prepare the vegetables for the evening meal. This was as much help as Mrs Welling would allow her to give, for the kitchen was her domain, and she was a very good cook.

Nothing else had been said about the unwanted help Thea was receiving, but it occupied both of their thoughts, and Thea could sense Mrs Welling's inward dilemma, and wished she would say something, and give her a chance to reinstate her case.

Her silent wish was granted just before she left Mrs Welling to get on with the dinner, having done as much as she was allowed to. 'Do you think I ought to thank Mr Conan for his help, Thea?' Mrs Welling asked in a rush of words, as if she had to get it out or bust.

Thea looked back at her. A wisp of her iron-grey hair had slipped out of its tightly-rolled bun and hung down her withered cheek. Thea took a deep breath, but managed to reply quite airily, in spite of the fury she felt building up inside her towards Marcus for putting her in such a position—and not only her, but this kind, fiercely independent old lady. 'Certainly not! We don't want to encourage him, do we?' she exclaimed. 'Besides,' she added with a weak smile, 'it's my fight, and I don't intend to lose. You can't go consorting with the enemy behind my back, not if you're on my side.'

CHAPTER FIVE

THE following week passed without incident. On the Wednesday, Sam did the carting of the cases to the kiosk, and Thea knew better than to try and stop him. He had been given his orders, and if he failed the chances were he would lose his job, and Thea did not want that on her conscience.

Although by now she had got used to the tall islander's presence, Thea still had that odd feeling that she was under surveillance. She had seen nothing of Marcus since he had appeared at Beach House, but Sam's presence was akin to having him around, and a constant reminder that she was still under Marcus's protective wing.

Far from being bored with the work, Sam made himself useful. Whenever Thea found herself inundated with a crowd of thirsty holidaymakers, she would find Sam beside her, cheerfully handing out cartons and requesting orders, and with a grin saying in that soft voice of his, 'You take the money, Miss John, I'll serve them.'

When this first happened, Thea wondered indignantly if Marcus was making a bid for the takeover of the kiosk, then her sense of humour came to her rescue and she accepted his help with an answering smile of thanks, and a feeling of weak resignation.

It wasn't really fair of Marcus to make his presence felt as much as this, she thought sadly, and it was not helping her to push him out of her life. He wouldn't see it that way, of course. His king-sized conscience over Michael's death would not allow him to, and it meant that she would have to go on receiving his help indefinitely, and the thought depressed her. Perhaps she ought to have married him and been done with it.

The very thought jerked her out of her miserable musings. What chance of happiness would either of them have? None at all, she told herself firmly, and however much she loved him, her pride would not accept such a proposition. As for her part in agreeing to marry him, she could only plead numb insensitivity. Michael's death had obviously robbed her of her normally sensible outlook, and Marcus must have known this and had taken advantage of her stupefied state, and that hadn't been fair of him either.

A week later Thea made the acquaintance of Timothy Saunders, an American in his late twenties who owned one of the small fishing boats that lay on the beach a few yards away from the kiosk.

She had only noticed him before at the weekends, when he would return from a fishing trip, and would always give her a companionable nod as he passed by the kiosk, but one day during the week he stopped to have a word with her, and was surprised at her very English accent, when she replied to a question of his about the heat of the day and how much cooler it was out there, nodding in the direction of the blue-green bay.

This had provoked other questions, such as what was she doing so far from home, and was she out to see the world, and remembering Pauline's comments on the wandering fraternity, Thea smiled and replied, 'Not exactly. I'm hoping to settle here.'

Tim had then ordered a Coke, and propped himself up on the ledge of the serving counter. 'Just
thought you'd like some sunshine for a change, was
that it?' he asked, his light blue eyes crinkling at the
corners of his well-tanned face.

Thea replied casually in the affirmative. She
knew he was curious about her, and had no intention of giving out any more information, but this
was not so easy, for his attitude was a friendly one
and not at all pushing and forward.

'We have an English club here,' he said, after
taking a long drink from his can. 'Sort of home from
home, so I understand,' he had volunteered. 'If
you're interested, I can put you in touch, or better
still, take you round one evening. I can vouch for a
rousing welcome for you, a new face is always welcome.'

Thea thanked him for his interest, but said that
she might consider joining such a club in time, but
she was a relative newcomer to the island and would
like to settle in first; then she tried to change the conversation by asking him if he had caught any fish.

He had grinned at this, and replied that he only
went out for the fresh air, and that wasn't an excuse,
because after being confined in a bank all day, he
needed peace from the eternal chatter of adding
machines and typewriters.

Out of the corner of her eye Thea could see that
Sam, who had settled himself in his favourite spot by
the side of the kiosk and who was supposed to be
immersed in a paper, had laid the paper down and
was openly inspecting her new acquaintance. If
Timothy Saunders had noticed this, he made no

comment on the fact. He was probably used to the ways of the indolent islanders, to whom time meant nothing, and not even the advent of tourism had managed to alter their simple philosophy that God had made the world and man had made time.

This attitude of watchfulness on Sam's part confirmed a suspicion of Thea's that his duties were not only confined to helping her with the rough work, but for her protection as well. However ludicrous it seemed, it was the only answer that made sense, although nothing else did. She was hardly the type to attract admirers and the day's takings did not amount to a vast sum liable to attract thieves, if the idea was to protect her from robbery.

On the Saturday, Tim made a point of stopping to have another chat to her on his way to the boat, and casually enquired if she had any off time, to which she had to reply that she had Sunday off, as Mrs Welling relieved her for that day, and she could have had an afternoon off in the middle of the week had she wanted it, but she preferred to be working. She still missed Marcus, and the only antidote for such yearnings was work and more work. Her first instinct to his query about free time was to say that she didn't need any off-time, the job was a holiday in itself, but he was bound to notice that she had Sunday off, particularly as he now made a point of having a word with her each time he came down to the beach and she had no wish to hand him a snub like that.

The next question was entirely predictable: would she care for a spin in the boat the following morning? and in spite of his casual invitation, Thea felt that she could not refuse the offer, but she warned him that she didn't know if she was a good sailor or not.

'It's as calm as a pond out there,' he had replied with a cheery grin. 'I'll pick you up about ten, how's that?' he told her. 'I don't know where you live,' he had added, just before he left her, 'or your name, come to that,' he apologised.

'I live just over there,' Thea replied, nodding in the direction of Beach House, 'and my name's Thea John.'

Timothy Saunders held out a hand towards her. 'I'm Tim Saunders- we seem to have got things the wrong way around, the introductions usually come first, don't they? Did you say John?' he queried as he shook her hand. 'That's odd, I used to know a Michael John,' he hesitated, then gave a light shrug. 'It's probably a common name anyway,' he added.

Thea withdrew her hand from his firm shake and looked towards the waves gently lapping the shore. What a small world it was, she thought sadly. Of all the people she had to meet it had to be someone who had known Michael. 'He was my brother,' she said quietly.

'You're Michael's sister?' he asked on a note of incredulity, then paused and shook his head slowly. 'So that's why you're out here. He did say something about his sister joining him, but after——' He hesitated, then fell silent.

'I arrived the day after the accident,' Thea explained. 'Otherwise I don't suppose I would have made the trip, there wouldn't have seemed any point,' she added sombrely.

Tim gave a great sigh. 'Gee, I wish I'd known you were here,' he said. 'It must have been hell to

walk in on that news.' He shook his head again as if
at a loss for words. 'I hadn't seen him for a fortnight, though, before it happened. I was away on
leave in Miami. Not that we saw that much of each
other, we used to meet up now and again for a drink
and a parley, and we'd see each other at local
flings.' He gave Thea a sympathetic look. 'So you
decided to stay on, then, did you?' he asked, and
flicked a quick eye over the interior of the kiosk.
'Not much of a job,' he commented. 'I'll see what I
can come up with in that line for you,' and as Thea
started to remonstrate he held up a silencing hand.
'Look, you're my buddy's sister, and that kind of
makes us related,' he grinned. 'You're not to worry
about a thing. I'll look out for you—Mike would
have done the same for any kid sister of mine,' he
added firmly.

Thea was worried, and her expression showed it
as she said hastily, 'Please, I know you mean well,
but I'm perfectly happy here, and I should hate any
other job. Look at the sunshine I get!' she added,
trying to sound jocular about it, and it didn't quite
come off as she was too concerned about proving her
point. She had enough trouble with Marcus looking
out for her, without adding another contender for
the post, in spite of her earlier wish to find just such
a person.

'What about free time?' Tim demanded. 'It's my
guess you don't get much of that.'

'I don't want a lot of free time,' Thea replied
quickly, then sighed. 'Not yet anyway,' she added
slowly. 'Surely you can understand that? I need
plenty of work, and this job suits me perfectly—if I
were offered any other work, I wouldn't take it,' she

ended firmly, her lovely wide grey eyes meeting the
doubtful ones of her companion.

Her last few words had settled the issue, Thea
found with no small relief as Tim replied softly,
'Okay, okay. We'll leave it at that for now.'

Shortly after that he left her, telling her to bring a
warm sweater with her the next morning as the sea
breezes could be chilly.

Thea's eyes followed his retreating back until he
was out of sight. She had a nasty feeling that things
were going to become very complicated, and wondered what it was about her that brought out the
protective instinct in the opposite sex. Tim had al-
luded to her as Mike's kid sister, and it was hardly a
fitting description of a twenty-two-year-old woman.
Marcus's attitude towards her had been exactly the
same, and Thea was getting a little tired of being
treated as if she didn't know how many beans made
five!

'Everything all right, Miss John?' Sam queried in
his soft voice.

Thea broke off from her indignant musings and
stared at Sam watching her with those large doleful
brown eyes of his.

'Yes, thank you, Sam,' she replied tartly, as if it
had been Marcus who had asked the question, then
relented as she saw his rather hurt expression at her
curt reply. 'That was a friend of my brother's,' she
explained carefully, thinking he might as well know
that, as it looked as if Tim was going to be around
quite a lot in the future, and it might be as well if
Marcus was informed of this fact. She was almost
sure that Sam had heard every word that had been
said, but she didn't know how much he would report

back to his boss, if indeed anything. Perhaps it was
enough that he was there and kept an eye on her.

When Mrs Welling heard that Thea had got
herself a nice boy-friend, as she called Timothy
Saunders, later the following morning when Thea
returned from her outing in his boat, to change into
a light suit ready to be taken out to lunch, Thea
was quick to point out that Timothy was only an
acquaintance, and certainly not a boy-friend, to
which Mrs Welling had given a knowing nod and
said that it was early days yet, and wasn't that him?
She had heard a car draw up outside the house.

A few minutes later Thea sat in Timothy's Fiat
and was whisked away from Beach House in a
manner that reminded her of her brother's approach
to driving, giving her an added insight to the man
seated beside her. She had learnt a lot about him
that morning on the boat trip, where she had received a short résumé of his life history—how he
came originally from a Miami bank to work in
Charlotte Amalie.

She knew that he was ambitious, and determined
to get on in his chosen career. 'The guys thought I
was crazy putting in for this post,' he had told her
with a smile, 'but I'm willing to bet I'll be a manager before I'm thirty, and that's more than you
could say of most of them.'

The more Thea learnt about Timothy, the less
she could see that he would have had in common
with her brother, apart from a natural aversion to
the responsibility of matrimony. Michael had
worked hard and played hard, and she supposed it
was that that had brought them together, but she
had a suspicion that Timothy had deliberately cul-

tivated Michael's company, for there had been an
underlying reference several times in the conversation he had had with her that morning, on the
wealth accumulation of some of the island's inhabitants, and how important it was to know the right
people who just might transfer their accounts to
another bank, preferably his. Thea had also learnt
the name of his bank, and knew that it was not the
bank that Michael had dealt with, or Marcus, for
that matter, for she had received a cheque from
Marcus for Michael's last month of work. With this
in mind it had not been too hard to guess what type
of client's accounts he was interested in, and she was
certain that Marcus would be one of them, very
probably the main one, for she knew that he was a
very wealthy man indeed.

When Timothy told her where he intended taking
her for lunch, her heart sank, for she had last visited
the Coral World, an underwater observatory, with
Marcus, and had had lunch with him in the restaurant leading to the entrance to the aquarium.

That was the trouble with small islands, she
thought sadly, this was the sort of thing that would
crop up with depressing regularity and she would,
she supposed, eventually get used to it, as she would
have to get over Marcus.

As with her visit to Mountain View with Pauline,
she told Timothy that she had previously visited the
aquarium on a sightseeing tour, adding quickly that
she looked forward to another visit. 'It's amazing,
isn't it,' she went on, 'to be able to glimpse the wonders of the deep. I don't think I'd ever get tired of
watching.'

This remark successfully turned Timothy's

thoughts away from her previous visit, and stopped him from enquiring who she had made the visit with, and that could have been awkward for Thea, who had no intention of mentioning her friendship with Marcus.

The two-hundred-and-fifty-seater restaurant was half full when they arrived, and Thea tried not to look towards the end of the restaurant where she and Marcus had sat on their visit, and was glad when they found a table near the entrance.

While they ate their lunch, a crabmeat salad for Thea, and a thick steak with salad on the side for Timothy, Thea found it hard to work up an appetite, for memories were crowding in on her just when she could least have done with them, and she wondered dismally if she really ought to consider going back to England, since there would be no poignant memories there to plague her existence— no anything, really, she thought bleakly, as she refused dessert, and wished she could get the rest of the visit over with in the shortest possible time. Meanwhile she resolved to refuse any further invitations from Timothy.

It wasn't that she had anything against him—in fact, if it hadn't been for her heartache over Marcus, he would have been the ideal companion for her, just the sort of person she had wished would turn up, for there would be no emotional ties here. He looked upon her as Mike's kid sister, as he had called her, and that was exactly how she would be treated, and that suited her fine, only she hadn't bargained for the memories such an alliance would bring. It was different with Pauline, of course, and she wished it was Pauline that she was sitting op-

posite to and not this friend of her brother's, who
was very kind, but somehow alien because he was
not the man she loved, and she very much doubted
if they would have much in common once the subject of Michael had been dismissed.

All these thoughts went through her head while
she answered Timothy's polite questions on her
background, and how well Michael had got on in
what was a very competitive career. 'I guess some
have it, and others haven't,' he had commented
with just a little envy in his voice. 'You have to be in
the right place at the right time, and he sure was
when he got that commission from Marcus Conan.'
Then realising that this was not a very tactful
remark to make, he hastily apologised.

Not liking the way the conversation was going,
Thea asked him about his background and again
successfully avoided having to answer any awkward
questions that might concern Marcus, since she was
certain that Timothy had no idea that she had once
been engaged to him.

Once lunch was over and they were in the aquarium, Thea felt much better. There was so much to
see and personal problems could be pushed aside.
They first ascended to the top of the three-tiered
building that gave a breathtaking view of the Atlan-
tic and the surrounding Virgin Islands, that could
just be seen through a heat haze in the distance, and
invariably the subject of the past was brought up
again, and Thea was forced to listen to her companion's remarks on the subject of piracy, that
somewhat differed from Marcus's comments, in that
Marcus had approached the subject from an histori-
cal angle and Timothy from a more material one,

such as the plunder the ships had been carrying, and how many vessels still lay on the ocean floor with the spoils of their rich cargoes waiting for some enterprising diving team to discover.

This completely different outlook between Marcus and Timothy Saunders only underlined Thea's feelings on somehow extricating herself from any future excursions in his company. If she hadn't still been in love with Marcus, she supposed she would have welcomed his interest in her, but as it was, she would only go on comparing the differences between the men, and that was not fair to Timothy, who was so keen on working his way up the ladder of success that it had coloured his outlook, and somewhere along the way he had picked up a cynical bitterness tinged with envy towards those who had made it.

They then descended from the upper level down to the second tier of the tower, and here was a man-made aquarium set in the walls surrounding the circular dome building, where the tropical fish glided by in brilliant splendour. The scorpion-fish that had caught Thea's eyes the last time she visited the aquarium again enthralled her. The brilliant, feathery-like deep pink corsaged display of its beauty almost hid the fact that it was a deadly species of its kind, and as Thea stood gazing at it, she was irresistibly reminded of Sapphire, and was glad when Timothy suggested that they move on down to the underwater observatory.

As this was the Coral World's main focal point, it was more crowded than the rest of the dome, and there was a lot of jostling for position, although the round chamber, fourteen feet beneath the surface of the sea, had ample viewing windows.

They spent less time here than in the other sec-
tions of the observatory because of the crowd, most
of whom were tourists, and who probably only had
this one opportunity of seeing a sea-diver's view of
the deep from a comfortable angle, and when Timothy, knowing that Thea had been before, suggested
that they get some fresh air, she willingly agreed and
made room for a small boy standing directly behind
her and left him staring at the wonders before his
eyes in open-mouthed absorption, and as Thea
moved away she heard him call out to someone a
little behind him, 'Look, there's a shark!'

In spite of Thea's earlier resolution of excusing
herself from any other invitation of Timothy's, she
found herself accepting his casual offer of making a
day of it, having tea out, and then taking her to one
of his favourite haunts, a bar on the outskirts of
Charlotte Amalie, where he had often met Michael
and several of his friends. If she was agreeable, that
was, and hadn't made any other arrangements for
the rest of the day?

Thea knew she ought to have snatched at the
chance offered, and said something about having
other plans, but her conscience would not allow her
to do so. It wasn't Timothy's fault that she had
made a fool of herself over a man who was way
beyond her reach, and it was time that she made a
positive effort to forget him. She was not going to do
it sitting with Mrs Welling in her cosy front parlour
each evening, relating her home life to the old lady,
who loved to hear about England, and who in
return would tell Thea of her own childhood. Thea
had no complaints about these evenings, as she

found them as absorbing as Mrs Welling did, but
she couldn't go on shutting herself away from other
company and Mrs Welling knew it, her pleasure in
the fact that Thea had found a gentleman friend
had borne witness to this salient fact.

After a light but refreshing tea, taken in a hotel
that overlooked the harbour, Timothy took Thea
back to Beach House so that she could tell Mrs
Welling of their plans, and that she wouldn't be
back until later that evening.

Had Thea previously had time to think about it,
she might have wondered what they would find to
talk about during the day's outing, but curiously
enough the time passed pleasantly by, with no awkward conversational pauses as might have been expected of two people who hardly knew one another,
and it struck Thea that Timothy would make an
exceptionally good bank manager as he obviously
had the gift of putting one at ease, an essential in-
gredient for success in that particular career.

Her own changed outlook had considerably
helped too, she admitted to herself as she recalled
her earlier feelings during lunch at the Coral World
when she had compared Timothy to Marcus and
made herself feel wretched. Now that she had
come to terms with this and decided to pull herself
out of her self-pity, for that was what it all really
amounted to, life began to look much brighter for
her, and she was able to congratulate herself on the
fact that she hadn't given Marcus a thought since
their visit to the Coral World.

The late afternoon and early evening period was
spent in a leisurely drive down to the harbour from
where they watched the activity of the busy port,

and from there to a vantage point on the hillside overlooking Drake's Passage where the cool breezes off the bay fanned Thea's cheeks and were a welcome relief from the heat of the town sector.

Soon the rays of the sinking sun were spread out before them like a fan of brilliant orange plumes across the water that reflected the image, and made Thea draw in a breath of sheer wonder at the sight, and banished all her good resolutions concerning Marcus for his image rose before her, and she wished with all her heart that he was there to witness this scene of perfect peace with her.

'Think you'll stay—permanently, I mean?' Timothy asked her, breaking into her unhappy musings.

Her hesitant, 'I don't know,' made him regret asking the question.

'It's early days yet, of course,' he said quickly. 'Time enough to think about things like that. Now I'll show you some of our night life,' he added with a grin.

The bar that Timothy took her to was in a hotel in the centre of Charlotte Amalie, and had only a few occupants when they first arrived. 'It'll get crowded later on,' he commented idly, after he had asked her what she would like to drink and Thea had requested a vodka and lime.

While they waited to be served, two more people arrived, a man and a woman, who walked across the room to a couple of stools at the other end of the bar and settled down to give their order. Timothy, whose eyes had followed their entrance, said quietly to Thea, 'Now there's a lucky girl,' and catching the dark-haired girl's eyes, waved a welcoming hand towards her that she acknowledged with a silent nod, and turned her attention back to her companion again. 'I ought to introduce you,' he went on, still in an undertone, 'but perhaps it's not convenient right now,' he added with a grin.

Thea glanced over to the girl again, wondering if she worked with Timothy or whether she was an old flame of his. She was very attractive and had a curvaceous figure, and was probably in her late teens, Thea surmised, and looked as if she knew her way around, because there was a certain air of sophistication about her.

Apart from this one glance, Thea took no further notice of the girl and gazed idly around the bar. Its low lighting from antique-looking ships' lanterns that hung on the walls around the room, and cutlasses with various other wicked-looking weapons, gave the bar a cosy if slightly sinister air.

The room was filling up now, and apart from a rush to get served at the bar, the loud chatter and gusts of laughter from the pushing crowd behind them made Thea hope that Timothy would suggest that they move on when they had finished the drinks that were just being pushed towards Timothy, but Timothy's next words took all such mundane thoughts out of Thea's mind. 'Fancy her taking up with old Johnson again,' he commented he paid for the drinks. 'I guess she's missing Michael,' he added in a low tone as if speaking to himself.

Thea's eyes went from him back to the girl. 'Did she know Michael?' she asked quickly.

Timothy nodded as he handed her her drink and picked up his change. 'There aren't many personable young men that our Dulcie doesn't know,' he replied. 'A lot depends on their bank balance and how generous they are with it.'

It took a moment or so for Thea to realise what he meant, and she looked away quickly from the girl and down to the drink in her hand. A vision of Michael then rose before her, and something he had said to her before going out one evening in his newly acquired sports car, after she had asked him to go steady, and complained that she didn't know why he was so addicted to fast cars. 'Not only fast cars, pet, but fast women as well—they go together,' he had said with a wicked grin.

Timothy gave her a quick searching look before saying quickly, 'Hell! I'm sorry. I ought to have kept my big mouth shut.'

Thea gave a half-shrug. 'It's all right,' she replied, giving him a twisted smile. 'You're not really telling me anything new. I was surprised, that's all,' she added, as she glanced back at the girl. 'You called her lucky, didn't you? Unless you meant that she's lucky that she's found someone else. As you said, she's probably missing Michael. He had a way with women.' She fixed her eyes on a large wicked-looking cutlass on the wall opposite her. 'I suppose it was because he was generous and good-natured.'

Timothy offered a cigarette which Thea refused. 'I was talking about the crash,' he said, after he had lit his cigarette. 'She was with Michael when it happened, and heaven only knows how she came out of it unscathed. She was badly shaken, of course, but no other injury.' He narrowed his eyes against the smoke of his cigarette. 'She was thrown clear, apparently.'

Thea's hand shook as she put her glass down on the table they had managed to find in the midst of the crowd. 'She was with Michael?' she asked in a shocked voice, and as Timothy turned and nodded towards an acquaintance at the bar, she repeated the question, adding urgently, 'Was she, Timothy?'

He gave her a surprised look. 'Didn't you know?' he said. 'Well, it wasn't a secret. I don't suppose it was necessary to tell you everything. I mean, hearing about the crash itself was bad enough for you. It was just one of those things. A friend of mine was at that party, and said afterwards that he thought Mike was a fool to take her with him. He saw them leaving, with poor old Mike half propping her to the car—that's the only thing with Dulcie, she gets high on a couple of drinks.'

'Michael used to be very careful about drinking and driving,' Thea said slowly, 'but as you said, it was just one of those things.'

'Mike wasn't drunk!' Timothy exclaimed in surprise. 'He wasn't that much of a fool. Besides, he was expecting to be called out by Mr Big.'

Thea's eyes left her hands that were clenched tightly together in her lap and she stared at Timothy. 'What did you say?' she asked slowly.

Timothy stubbed his cigarette out before answering her. 'Mr Big?' he replied. 'Oh, that's just a name for the man he worked for, Marcus Conan, the property tycoon he was designing some flats for.'

Thea shook her head in an impatient action. 'No, not that,' she said. 'What did you say about Michael not being drunk?' she demanded fiercely.

Timothy's eyebrows rose. 'Look,' he said quietly, 'let's forget it, shall we? I'm a clot for bringing it up again like that.'

'Please, Timothy, it's important to me,' Thea said urgently.

For a split second it looked as if he was not going to oblige, but after taking one look at Thea's earnest expression he sighed and said abruptly, 'Okay. Well, you know how it is when anything like that happens. The whole thing gets chewed over. We were all pretty shaken at the news. I heard about it as soon as I got back from leave. John, this friend of mine—well, friend of both of us, Mike as well, I mean—was at this party and I got the info from him. If Mike was half cut he'd have said so, but as I said, he knew Conan would want to see those plans that night. John overheard him telling Jack—he was the guy who was giving the party—that he would probably be called out during the evening.'

Thea drew in a quick breath. 'So there was no reason why M—Mr Conan should feel partially responsible, then?' she said, more to herself than to her companion.

Timothy's brows lifted. 'Now where did you hear that?' he queried in surprise.

'Oh, it was just an impression I got when he told me about Michael,' she replied slowly, and looked up from her glass that she had studiously studied in order not to show her companion how much his news had affected her. 'He met me at the airport, you see,' she explained carefully.

Timothy nodded his understanding. 'Well, you're wrong there,' he replied firmly. 'Sure, he must have been shaken, we all were, but it's my guess he laid the blame elsewhere.' His eyes rested briefly on the woman he had named as Dulcie, and who was now staring dolefully into her glass.

'Dulcie?' queried Thea, her eyes following his glance.

'She didn't get much sympathy from him, I gather,' he replied as he picked up his glass and took a drink from his rye-on-the-rocks. 'Probably overdid the thank-you act later, hoping to cash in on the acquaintance. He was first on the scene,' he told Thea. 'He'd been waiting for Mike at the corner of the drive-in to his place, and he heard the crash.'

Thea blanched visibly at the thought of Marcus coming upon a scene like that.

'Look, are you sure you want to go over this?' Timothy demanded.

'I'm sure,' Thea replied firmly.

Timothy gave her a hard look, then gave a half-shrug and lit another cigarette before starting again. It was plain that he could not understand Thea's insistence on discussing such a morbid subject. 'As I said, he was first on the scene. If he hadn't heard the crash, he would have heard Dulcie. I'm told she sat in the middle of the road wailing like a demented banshee—half the island must have heard her.' He took another swallow of his drink. 'So Conan takes charge—gets her off to hospital and off the scene.' It was then that an idea occurred to him that made him break off abruptly and stare at Thea. 'I'm only telling you this to show you you must have got the wrong impression from Conan. You've not got a grudge against him, have you?' he asked casually, but with the light of speculation in his eyes, then went on before Thea could reply, 'I've an idea that Dulcie tried on some sort of touch, but he dealt with her fast enough and told her in no uncertain terms to stay off the drink if she couldn't handle it.'

Thea's eyes widened at the implication behind his words. 'I've no such thing in mind!' she got out quickly, her lovely eyes showing her distress that he should think such a thing of her.

'Perish the thought!' Timothy replied hastily. 'I've put my big foot in it again, haven't I? It's just that I wouldn't blame you if you had. I just wanted to put you straight, that's all. A man like that is no pushover. Great as a friend, but as an enemy— you've got trouble with a capital T.'

It was hard after this for Thea to concentrate on anything else but the news Timothy had given her about her brother's accident, and she was relieved when some friends of Timothy's joined them and she was introduced to them. Apart from their first condolences over the loss of her brother, other topics were soon introduced and the evening passed quickly by for Thea, who was impatient to get back to Beach House and the privacy of her room, so that she could make some sense of what she had been told, and why Sapphire had given her another version of the story—and above all, why Marcus hadn't attempted to refute her accusation that he was only marrying her to salve his conscience over what had happened to her brother.

CHAPTER SIX

THEA got back to Beach House shortly after ten, and after letting herself in with a key Mrs Welling had given her, made her way to her room, answering Mrs Welling's 'Is that you, Thea?' as she passed her bedroom.

While she took a cool shower, her mind was busy working out the implications of what she had heard that night. It was obvious that Sapphire had not known about Dulcie—or that Marcus thought that she was to blame for the accident. She lifted her face towards the welcoming cool spray of water. Perhaps she had known, Thea thought, and had chosen to ignore that part of it in her bid to get Thea out of Marcus's life.

Her smooth forehead creased in a frown as she thought of Marcus and his refusal to even discuss the matter with her, as if it didn't matter, she thought sadly. It hadn't, of course, to him. He cared so little about her he had let her go on thinking that he blamed himself for Michael's death.

After hurriedly towelling herself down she went back into her room. If it hadn't been his conscience that had made him propose, what had it been? she asked herself distractedly. Pity? She gave a deep sigh. That was it, of course, and it was a much worse reason than the other one in Thea's eyes. No one likes to be pitied. 'You'll have a beautiful house, lovely clothes. Nothing's going to be too good for you,' Sapphire's jeering words pierced through Thea's consciousness, 'but you won't have his love.'

Thea put her hands to her ears in a vain attempt to shut out these heartrending remarks. It would have been better if she hadn't learned the truth, she told herself; she would at least have been spared this second humiliation.

A ragged sob escaped her as she got into bed. No, she had had to know, she told herself. That way it was easier to face up to the unpalatable fact that she had been living in a dream.

Marcus knew that she had fallen in love with him, he was too experienced in those matters not to know, and had not had the heart to push her out of his life. A teardrop slipped down her cheek and she brushed it away angrily. It would have been much kinder if he had. He would know just how to do it; she wasn't that insensible and was bound to have got the message that he wasn't interested in her, not in that way.

Was that why he had sent Sapphire to the hotel, she wondered, to let her know that he was not suffering from any pangs of rejection? She recalled again the way he had looked towards the reception desk before looking for Sapphire, and Thea was sure that he had known that she was on duty. He didn't have to pick Sapphire up there. He could have arranged to meet her elsewhere. She gave a deep sigh. And wasted the chance of showing Thea that he was not short of feminine company—oh, no, it was too good a chance to miss. Since she had removed herself from his social circle there had been no other way that he could rub the fact in, she thought sadly.

But why should he bother? she asked herself bewilderedly. Was it his ego that needed soothing? He must have received a shock when she had returned his ring—or tried to, as she thought of the opulent ring now lying in her dressing-table drawer. Sapphire had bitterly pointed out that he was not the marrying type, so why should he plague her with these attentions?

She leaned over and switched off her bedside lamp. What possible reason could he have for keeping tabs on her? she wondered crossly, and shook her head. It didn't make sense, none of it did—unless— her eyes opened wide as a probable explanation hit her. So it was conscience after all! Not through what had happened to Michael, but the way he had led her up the proverbial garden path! She had made no secret of the fact that she knew that he didn't love her, and the rest had not needed spelling out.

She sank slowly back on to her pillows. It had taken her a long time to get there, but now things started to add up. Marcus must have felt a heel, and was now trying to make up for it in the only way he knew how, by watching over her. Money was no worry to him, hence the appearance of Sam whom he was paying to just hang around the kiosk all day as a personal watchdog.

Her hand clenched on the counterpane. There was nothing she could do about it except put up with it, whether she liked it or not and she didn't like it. It would do no good to move on. Wherever she went he would find her, she thought, recalling his fury at her for not telling him she was leaving the hotel. It was such a small island that she couldn't hope to simply drop out of sight, and that meant that she would have to accept his unasked-for assistance until she either moved on to another island or went back to the U.K.

Her eyes were dimmed by tears of frustration. She had done nothing to warrant finding herself in such an unenviable position. All she had wanted was to be left alone to try and make another life for herself. She did not need a guardian, or a keeper, and she did not want to move on. She was happy with Mrs Welling, and Marcus's interference had almost cost her her job. 'Stay out of my life, Marcus Conan!' she whispered fiercely in the silence of her room.

His answering, 'I never make a promise that I don't intend to keep,' echoed through her drowsy mind before she fell asleep, but she was too tired to work out the implication behind this remark.

During the following week Timothy rang her up on the Tuesday evening. He knew of a party taking place at a friend of his the following evening, and how about it? Thea was apologetic but very firm. She did not care much for parties, but was careful not to expound on this theme, and thanked him anyway for thinking of her. To her relief he accepted her refusal with, 'Guess you're not ready to live it up yet. Don't get yourself tied up for the weekend, though,' he added before he rang off.

By the time Saturday dawned Thea was actually looking forward to seeing Timothy again. Her feelings had fluctuated alternately during the week. At times she would feel a positive urge to get out and about and at least try to make up her mind about her future.

It was all very well telling herself that she was going to stay put, but where would that get her? She was sensible enough to know that the job she had, although very pleasant, was hardly going to provide her with enough money to live on should she suddenly decide to move on.

If she was not very careful, she told herself firmly, she would end up as one of the drifters Pauline had told her about, with no particular goal in life, only an odd kind of waiting to see what lay behind the next bend. It was all too easy to adopt such an attitude in this lovely tropical playground, but time would slip by and would erode her determination to pull herself out of her lethargy.

These thoughts had so frightened Thea that she had made a pact with herself. She would give herself just six months and no more. She knew that Mrs Welling was seriously considering accepting an offer from her nephew to housekeep a flat he had decided to purchase, which would give her a home and would ease the domestic chores she had coped with at Beach House. As for Beach House, it had been suggested that a manager be put in, although as Mrs Welling had confided to Thea, a manager was rather a grand term for such a small boarding house, and ideally it should be a widow like herself, but much younger, of course, and able to cope with the daily routine.

'But that's all in the future, my dear,' she had ended. 'If Andy had wanted me to sell up and move in with him, then I wouldn't have considered it, as he very well knew,' she had added with a smile. 'As it is, I shall be able to keep an eye on things and make certain that none of my guests suffer from the changeover. We shall keep the kiosk as well, of course, that's been in the family for more years than

I care to remember.'

Thea was certain that there had been a message behind these confidences of Mrs Welling, and she had been telling her that she was not to feel obliged to stay on for her sake and should a suitable vacancy turn up then she should go ahead and take it.

In fact, they were both marking time, Thea thought dryly, and suspected that the first move would have to come from her. She had felt a glow of warmth towards the old lady who while appreciating Thea's company had known that the job was only a stopgap for her.

As she carried the tray of rolls down to the kiosk that Saturday morning, her spirits were higher than they had been for several days, and she resolved to accept any invitation that Timothy threw her way. She had been through a bad time and surely things must look up from now on.

When she had opened the kiosk and carried the tray of food through, she busied herself by preparing for the rush that was sure to come during the afternoon, and as she worked she hummed a cheerful ditty to herself. First she arranged the food in a tempting display under the glass-covered container, and when this was done she got out a fresh box of straws. She was always running out of straws, she thought as she placed the box within easy reach of the customers.

Her arms, she noted with satisfaction, had now turned a pleasant honey shade, and no longer gave her away as a raw newcomer to the island. For the sake of coolness she wore a bikini-top type of outfit with matching shorts that fitted snugly to her slim slight figure. It was an outfit that she wouldn't have dared to wear during her first week, but she had soon found herself surrounded by the sunbathing fraternity, the men and boys in swimming trunks, and the women in wisps of bikinis that made Thea's suntop look very respectable.

After a swift glance around her, Thea decided she was ready for business and opened the front of the kiosk, then frowned as the thought struck her that something was wrong but she couldn't put her finger on it. Then she had it: Sam was missing! She gave a quick glance towards the spot he always occupied and lifted her brows in surprise when she saw no sign of him.

Her first thought was one of slight dismay. She had got so used to his silent but extremely helpful company, particularly when she was extra busy, and she wondered how she was going to cope on her own.

A moment later she was chiding herself for her thoughtlessness. He might be ill, she thought, then drew in her breath sharply—or had Marcus called off his watchdog?

Thea felt a sense of keen disappointment at this thought. It hadn't taken him long to lose interest, she thought sadly, and wondered if the appearance of Timothy had anything to do with it, and if she was right, then Sam must have made a very full report back to his boss.

If Marcus had decided to call him off, why had he to pick a weekend, she wondered crossly, just when she could have done with some help!

She served a small boy with a can of fruit juice and a packet of biscuits, with a slight frown on her face that must have made him wonder if he had got

the right money to pay for his purchases, but her
thoughts were far away from such mundane matters.
It was no help telling herself that she had been lucky
in having anyone to help her. The kiosk had always
been run by one person before, and if people got
impatient when they had to wait in a queue—well,
they had just had to put up with it, they were all
served eventually, but thanks to the interference of
Marcus Conan, Thea had not been given the opportunity of coping on her own with a rush of
customers.

Well, it wouldn't be long before she made up for
this lack of experience, she thought somewhat ap-
prehensively as she saw a steady line of sunbathers
converging on her from different directions.

Soon she was engulfed in the business of serving
the thirsty customers, and stopping to put layers of
mustard on hamburgers already well laced with the
strong condiment, at special requests, a task she
could well have done without at that time.

'Will those who just want drinks line up this side,'
said a voice that automatically commanded attention and made Thea almost drop the pot of mustard
she was holding, and stare incredulously at Marcus
as he stationed himself beside her in the kiosk,
adding with a brisk, 'Now who's next?'

It was no time for an argument, but she couldn't
help exclaiming, 'Marcus! What on earth do you
think you're doing?'

His lifted brows as he calmly continued to serve
the cans of fruit juice proved her question to be utterly irrelevant, and she quickly turned her attention back to the job in hand.

For the next fifteen minutes Thea remembered

taking orders and automatically providing the food, conscious the whole time of the nearness of Marcus, of his sureness and strength, and the wonder of his presence. It had been a fortnight since she had seen him, and as the crowd thinned and gradually dispersed, leaving them alone, she knew an absurd longing to throw herself into his arms and cry her heart out, and if he still wanted to marry her then she would shout the word 'Yes!' for all the world to hear.

Her candid eyes, that gave so many of her thoughts away, dropped to the counter as they met the searching green ones of Marcus. She was ashamed of her weakmindedness where he was concerned, and dismayed to find that his absence had only made her love him more and she had desperately missed him.

To cover her misery she took refuge in indignation. 'I could have managed,' she commented waspishly. 'They would have had to wait.'

Marcus said nothing but continued to look at her, and Thea felt her cheeks grow warm under his steady scrutiny. She also found herself wishing she was not dressed so skimpily as his eyes flicked almost casually over her bare shoulders and rested for a second on her bikini top. 'I would prefer you to wear a blouse—or a dress,' he commented quietly.

Thea's eyes grew wide and her cheeks turned a deeper shade of red. How dare he tell her what to wear! Did he tell Sapphire what to wear? she wondered caustically, and at this thought her fury abated. He was probably buying her clothes anyway, so he wouldn't have to. This thought made her want to hit out at him and want to hurt him as much as he had hurt her. 'And to what do I owe the pleasure of your company?' she asked caustically, completely ignoring his remark about her dress.

His eyes narrowed as he acknowledged the snub she had handed out to him, but his voice was calm enough as he replied casually, 'I've missed you, but I don't suppose you'll believe that,' and went on, after giving a slight nod in confirmation of Thea's sceptical look at this statement, 'I rather thought we might have dinner together. I've given Sam the day off and decided to lend a hand. I gather the weekend is your busy time.'

Thea saw more customers approaching and hurriedly said, 'I suppose I can't stop you staying on to help, but I'm afraid dinner's out. I'm more or less committed for the weekend.'

She saw Marcus's lips firm at this refusal of hers to become embroiled in his private life again, but she had no intention of weakening on this point. His sudden arrival had only served to emphasise her longing for his company, and his invitation was only a gesture on his part to satisfy himself that she had forgiven him for what had happened.

She sighed inwardly as she served out more food. If only she could accept his company for one evening, if only to prove to him that he didn't have to go on making this kind of gesture—but she couldn't; she daren't.

Why couldn't he see what he was doing to her? Was he so caught up with his own feelings of remorse that he couldn't or wouldn't stay out of her life? What more could she do to make him understand? she wondered miserably.

'What exactly do you mean by "more or less

committed for the weekend"?' Marcus asked her as
soon as they were alone again.

Thea took a deep breath and stared at the box of
straws in front of her and absently thought that she
ought to replenish it again. She kept her glance
there, refusing to meet Marcus's searching stare.
'What I said,' she replied firmly. 'I was asked to
keep the weekend free.'

'By whom?' Marcus queried persistently, making
her draw in another breath and pray for patience.

'By a friend of mine,' she snapped back, as her eyes
met his defiantly. 'I thought we'd agreed to——'
She hesitated here, then began again, 'Well, you
know what I'm talking about, don't you? I just can't
understand why you bother to——' She took another deep breath. 'I'm very grateful for what
you've done for me, but honestly you don't have to
go on feeling that you owe me anything, because
you don't. What happened is in the past, and I'd
like it kept that way. I see no point in renewing the
association,' she ended lamely. If he hadn't got the
message now, he would never get it, she thought.

Marcus's green eyes blazed searingly into hers,
and Thea almost took a step back in amazement.
Somewhere along the line she had touched upon a
raw spot, and she had no idea where. His pride,
perhaps. There wouldn't be many women who
would tell him to get lost in so many words, she
thought miserably, although she hadn't meant to
put it so baldly, but she had no other way of com-
municating her feelings to him. He had left her no
choice in the matter, other than telling him outright
that she loved him desperately and she couldn't take
any more.

'I get the message,' he said savagely in a voice
that Thea had never heard him use before. 'I've
stood a lot from you, honey, but now I think it's
time that we came to another understanding. You're
right, I don't owe you a thing, but you owe me a
hell of a lot. You accept my proposal and the next
day you change your mind. What sort of a man do
you think I am?' he demanded harshly. 'Okay, so
you don't want marriage, so that was my mistake. I
thought you wouldn't settle for less, and I could
have sworn——' He broke off abruptly and laid a
long lean forefinger on her bare shoulder and slowly
traced the line of her honey-coloured flesh to her
slim neckline, making Thea shiver in apprehension.
He had never touched her like that before and she
felt like a wanton he had just picked up. 'Just out for
a good time, are you?' he asked her softly. 'I can
give you that with no strings attached, if that's what
you want.'

Thea's wide eyes mirrored her distress. 'Marcus,
please!' she whispered. 'Don't talk like that,' she
pleaded. 'You know it's not like that at all.'

'I know nothing of the sort!' he bit back at her
savagely. 'So you'll have to teach me, won't you? I
guess that's what got me about you from the start.
You were so damned innocent—or appeared so.
You don't know much about men, that's for sure,
and sooner or later you're going to land yourself into
trouble, honey. I wouldn't advise you to flutter your
big eyes at anyone else the way you did with me. As
hardbitten as I am, I thought it was for real, and I
thought I knew all the tricks! You can tell whoever
it is that you've promised to keep the weekend free
for that someone else has a prior claim on your com-

pany. Got it? I'm calling the tune from now on.' His
hard eyes met Thea's startled ones. 'If you don't
believe me, go ahead and keep that other date,' he
threatened harshly.

Thea felt like shaking her head to clear her senses.
This was not the man she knew but someone
entirely different, a hard, uncompromising man who
was determined to get his own way, and she didn't
care at all for the way his hard eyes were boring into
hers as if to bend her to his will.

With an effort she managed to tear her eyes away
from his compelling gaze. 'Very well,' she replied
quietly. 'I shall have dinner with you. There was no
need to threaten me,' she added with quiet dignity
as her candid eyes met his. 'I'm sorry you should
feel it necessary to use that sort of coercion on me—
and you're right, of course, I am in debt to you,' she
added wearily.

Marcus's eyes narrowed at her cold admission,
but he did not apologise. 'We'll dine at home,' he
announced grandly, and it took Thea back to their
earlier acquaintance when they had often had dinner at his flat, and she had loved the quiet intimate
evenings. She gave a slight shiver as the meaning
of his harsh words flowed over her. 'I thought you
wouldn't settle for less than marriage.'

The arrival of more customers was a very welcome break for Thea, whose shocked senses had left
her numb and utterly defenceless against such a
man as Marcus Conan, but she would keep her
word, she told herself dully; she owed him that
much, and before the evening was through he was
going to find out a few home truths, she promised
herself grimly, and she very much doubted if he

would bother to haunt her existence after that.

As the crowd thinned out she saw Timothy striding towards them and drew in a deep breath of
dismay. She had entirely forgotten about Timothy,
and she didn't want Marcus to meet him, particularly in the sort of mood he was in—and when
he found out that Timothy was the man who——
She swallowed convulsively. There was nothing she
could do about it now, she thought despondently as
she watched him stride the last few yards to the
kiosk, his eyes not on Thea but on Marcus, who was
watching his approach with narrowed eyes, and it
suddenly struck Thea that he knew who Timothy
was, and why he had picked that day to help her
out in the kiosk.

'Hi!' Timothy greeted her, his light blue eyes resting on Thea and then on her companion, embracing
both of them in the greeting, and Thea now knew
that Timothy knew Marcus. There wouldn't be
many island folk who didn't, she thought crossly,
and wondered how she was going to explain the
reason for Marcus's presence in the kiosk.

As it happened no explanation was called for. She
did attempt to introduce the men to each other,
Marcus intervened with, 'It's Saunders, isn't it? I
believe I saw you at the conference last week,
didn't I?'

Timothy beamed at the recognition. 'That's right,
sir,' he said. 'The manager couldn't make it. I
thought your summing up of the future trend of tourism was pretty accurate,' he added enthusiastically,
with overtones of respect that made Thea want to
stamp her foot in temper as she acknowledged the
salient fact that Marcus would receive no opposition

from Timothy as far as she was concerned, in spite
of the fact that he was obviously mystified by
Marcus's presence in the kiosk.

Marcus soon settled his doubts by announcing
calmly, 'I've come to keep an eye on my girl,' giving
Timothy a look that plainly said that he was wasting
his time if he had hopes in that direction.

After giving a quick startled nod at this thinly
veiled warning, Timothy said hurriedly, 'Well, I
suppose I'd better get the old girl shipshape if I
want to catch the tide,' and with a vague cheery
wave he moved on towards his boat.

'That was a rotten thing to do!' Thea exclaimed
angrily. 'I'm not your girl now, so why did you lie
to him?' she demanded.

'Because he would have found out sooner or later,
and I prefer it to be sooner. At least he's got plenty
of time to make other arrangements for the weekend
now,' Marcus said casually.

Thea stared at him. 'You knew it was Timothy,
didn't you?' she said flatly, then looked back at
where Timothy was making the preparations for his
trip out to the bay. 'He was a friend of Michael's,'
she said slowly, and her voice shook a little as she
added, 'He didn't have any ulterior motive in getting to know me. He just wanted to look out for me,
for Michael's sake.' Her voice petered out miserably.
'I wonder what he thinks of me now,' she added, as
she stared at her small clenched hands resting on the
counter.

Marcus tilted her head up with a gentle forefinger
and looked down at her. 'Okay!' he said abruptly.
'So I'll make it up to him. I could do with a bright
young accountant.'

Thea swallowed, and resisted the urge to lay her head on that strong shoulder of his as she had done so often before when grief had overcome her. He didn't understand, she thought unhappily, he would never understand. Everything could be solved by money in his eyes, and the thought that Timothy would probably jump at the chance of working for him did not lessen her misery for one minute.

CHAPTER SEVEN

WHEN they closed the kiosk at six o'clock, Marcus made it plain that he had no intention of leaving Thea at Beach House and returning later for her, but intended to spend the early evening period with her too, and that meant that Thea had to introduce him to Mrs Welling, who at first was a little flustered by his august presence, but under his skilful and sure touch with the opposite sex, be they young or old, she was soon chattering away to him as if they had known each other for years.

It was small wonder that he had done so well in the hotel trade, Thea thought scathingly as she took a shower and freshened herself up before Mrs Welling prepared their tea for them, and she wondered what Mrs Welling would think if she knew that behind that charming, handsome façade of Marcus Conan lay a ruthless character who had surely been born in the wrong century. He belonged to the age of the cutlass, and it didn't take much imagination on Thea's part to see him jumping out of the long-boat on to the shore swinging a murderous-looking weapon before him and with a look in his eye that spelt death to any luckless soul in his path.

She shivered as she slipped a cool dress over her head. He might have American nationality, but he was where he belonged, there was no doubt of that. The darker undertones of the islands' history were not only in his blood, but in his outlook too. Whatever he wanted, he would take, one way or another. With his looks and autocratic bearing plus a well-filled wallet, he could be certain of success.

She stared at her reflection in the dressing table mirror. What on earth had he seen in her? she wondered. She was no beauty to send his senses reeling—or any man's, come to that. Her head went to one side as she studied herself. He had said she was different, she recalled, and had then accused her of playing with him—fluttering her big eyes at him was the way he had put it. She closed her eyes at the memory of those idyllic days and cosy evenings with him not so very long ago. She had been so much in love with him that it wouldn't have occurred to her to use any wiles or any form of flirtation on him.

She gave a deep sigh as she laid her hairbrush down on the table top. Yes, she was different. Different from the women he had known, in that she was simple and incredibly naïve. Sapphire had had all the answers, and Thea was indebted to her and very thankful that she had acted on her advice. She doubted that the 'engagement' would have got as far as the altar, not if a certain event had taken place before the wedding. Her cheeks flamed at this thought. It could have happened that way, she told herself, and it was no use burying her head in the sand and refusing to acknowledge this fact. Her lips firmed as she prepared to join Marcus and Mrs Welling in the lounge. Forewarned is forearmed, she told herself as she lifted her head high and went down to join them.

Before they left for Pirates' Cove, Thea changed into an evening dress, since although they were having dinner in Marcus's flat, she knew that afterwards they would sit out on the hotel's floodlit terrace, and that was another part of the past that had painful memories for her.

How different it would all be now, she told herself wistfully as she got into Marcus's car and waved to the immensely satisfied-looking Mrs Welling, who had seen her guest to the door and ordered Thea to enjoy herself. Would those large beautiful stars that had shone down upon her in what now seemed a century ago still fill her with a sense of infinity, or would they appear as cut-out images pasted on a board of velvet? she wondered, as the sleek car purred its way along the beach road towards the hotel.

Marcus was silent as he concentrated on his driving, and Thea was glad of this. He was content, it seemed, that he had managed to get his own way so far with her, but if he had any other plans in line then he was in for a big disappointment. This would be the last time she would see him—well, alone, that was—and she was going to make that clear too before the evening was through.

Before long they were drawing up in the hotel car park, and Marcus, getting out and assisting Thea to alight, grinned at her. 'That's what I like about you,' he said in amusement. 'I don't know of any other woman who waits for me to open the door for her—or that I would bother to, come to that,' he added musingly. 'With you, it's a kind of natural action.'

He pulled her hand through his arm as they walked towards the hotel reception area. 'You don't chatter, either,' he added thoughtfully, 'and you've no idea how much I've missed that.'

Thea gave him a wary side glance, but still said nothing. She was wondering if she was going to spend the evening receiving compliments, no doubt with a certain purpose in mind, she thought dryly, but it wasn't going to work, and it was almost a shame to disappoint him.

The dinner was well up to the usual standard that Thea had become used to, and she took particular notice of the fact that her favourite menu had been served right down to the sweet course, a rich chocolate cake filled with fresh cream, reminding her of a past remark of Marcus's that he didn't know anybody else who would have dared to indulge in such fare as they were too afraid of putting on weight.

Thea had never envisaged a time when she would long for the end of an evening in his company, a complete end, that was, to everything that had gone before. She had done with star-gazing, and the evening was turning out much as she had envisaged, as a re-run of an old movie. The magic had gone, leaving her feeling depleted and somehow jaded, and she was beginning to hate Marcus for spoiling her dream world. It was certainly a much better world than she was in now, she told herself sadly, as Marcus guided her to his private alcove on the terrace after dinner.

The alcove was situated at the far end of the hotel, and was more in the nature of an arbour, with climbing shrubs nestling along the trellis work that formed a barrier that effectively separated the alcove from the rest of the terrace, but left the occupants a full view of the scenic panorama spread out before them, for the hotel was built on a hill that overlooked the bay that was part of the holiday complex.

The alcove was large enough to contain an ornate garden table and two chairs of matching style, and Thea's first thought was how many women Marcus had entertained there during the years, and the thought surprised her. She had sat there so often in the past and not once had such a thought occurred to her.

She had been very slow, she thought ironically, but she was learning fast, and she thanked the waiter who had appeared silently with a tray of drinks and then left as unobtrusively as he had come, leaving Marcus to mix the drinks.

Thea watched him pick up the cocktail shaker in his strong well-shaped hands and start to mix her Martini, and her mind went back to the night that he had proposed to her and she frowned. In view of what she now knew about him it was entirely out of character. He had said that he saw no other way— She felt her cheeks grow warm and was grateful for the dimmed light around her, but it still didn't make sense. He had so much going for him, and it wasn't as if he loved her, so why had he proposed?

'Why did you ask me to marry you, Marcus?' she asked casually, as she accepted the glass he held out towards her.

Marcus gave her a quick assessing look before he sat down opposite her and drew his glass towards him. 'I told you,' he replied, just as casually. 'Anything else you want to know?' he asked lightly.

'That doesn't answer my question,' Thea replied quietly. 'So I'm green and inexperienced, that's really what you mean, isn't it? You felt you couldn't take advantage of me, was that it?' she asked.

'I guess it's what it boils down to,' he replied dryly.

Thea shook her head bewilderedly. 'But why marriage?' she asked.

'Wasn't that what you wanted?' he asked her bluntly. 'Would you have settled for less?'

'Not if you mean what I think you mean,' she replied indignantly.

He gave a half-shrug of his powerful shoulders. 'That's what I figured,' he said slowly.

'For goodness' sake!' Thea exclaimed impatiently. 'Are you honestly telling me that you were prepared to tie yourself down for life on a whim—just because you——' She swallowed; she couldn't go on, and he knew very well what she meant.

Marcus's eyes opened a fraction wider at her cool reasoning. 'Who said it was for life?' he asked in a voice that showed his amazement.

Thea felt her throat constrict. 'How long exactly do you think it would last?' she heard herself asking.

She received another piercing stare from him, then he gave another shrug of his shoulders that fitted his evening jacket so perfectly. 'How the hell do I know the answer to that?' he replied somewhat irritably, as if she had asked a stupid question. 'Maybe a year, maybe two,' his mocking eyes met Thea's widening ones. 'We might set a record and make it five,' he added softly. 'Having second thoughts, are you?'

This was asked in a tone of utter sureness, and with mocking undertones that said that he might have changed his mind since, and Thea wanted to slap his arrogant face, but she wasn't finished yet. She couldn't believe any of this conversation, and wondered if she was dreaming. It was a little akin to hitting one's head against a stone wall, it was nice when you stopped. 'And afterwards?' she queried breathlessly. 'When the attraction has worn off, because that's what you mean, isn't it?'

He gave a deep sigh as if to say that he didn't think such information was necessary at that stage of the game. 'The same as happens to everybody else,' he replied harshly. 'You go your way, and I go mine. You'll have no need to worry about the future. I shall provide for you, you'll have all you could possibly want, and please yourself what you do with your time.' His white teeth gleamed in the dim light. 'Like a rich widow,' he added, 'only you'll be a rich divorcee.'

'I know this is a stupid question,' she said quickly, 'but what about children?'

He scowled at her. 'Children are fine, as long as they're someone else's,' he replied curtly. 'Does that answer your question?'

Thea nodded. She had got the picture now. 'Do you know why I turned you down?' she asked, as steadily as she was able, for she could feel the fury rising within her at the thought that she had very nearly married this overbearing, utterly selfish man. She must have been mad to fall in love with him in the first place. She had needed a drastic cure, and she had got one, she thought grimly.

'Sure,' he replied dryly. 'You thought I was marrying you to make up for what happened to your brother.'

Thea gave a decisive shake of her head, then took a deep breath. 'Well, I suppose that was part of it,' she conceded slowly, 'but I wouldn't have turned you down on that basis alone. I asked you if you loved me, if you remember— and you dodged the issue.'

Marcus's autocratic brow lifted at this. 'I wouldn't know the meaning of the word,' he drawled. 'Sure, I know all that stuff about love making the world go round, but in my book it's overrated. So is marriage. It only serves to give an aura of respectability to what after all is said and done is a natural instinct. The happy-ever-after cliché is a myth, and the stuff for dreamers— and I guess you're one of them, honey,' he ended mockingly.

Thea looked away from the amusement in his eyes, her heart felt as heavy as lead. 'That's what Sapphire said,' she replied in a low voice. 'She knows you well, doesn't she?' She stood up suddenly, wanting to remove herself as far as possible away from this despicable man. 'You ought to thank your lucky stars that I didn't marry you, Marcus,' she said in a low vibrant voice. 'I'm everything that you despise. Yes, I'm a dreamer. I believe in marriage and the happy-ever-after bit. I also believe in children, and wouldn't contemplate marriage without them. I suggest you marry Sapphire, I'd say you were well suited!' She swept her evening bag off the table in a manner that showed her disdain for him, and the need to remove herself from his company. 'Don't bother to see me home,' she announced grandly. 'I'll pick up a taxi on the stand,' and marched off.

She felt Marcus's eyes on her as she walked out of the arbour and towards the hotel car park only a few yards away from the front of the hotel. When she reached the line of taxis she got in the first one she came to, and was about to give her address to the cabby, when a hard voice cut across the stillness of the night. 'Move off that spot and you're fired!'

With mounting fury Thea heard the cabby's reply of, 'Yes, sir!' and put up the 'for hire' sign again that he had lowered when she had got in the cab, and she glared at Marcus as he opened her door. 'I brought you, and I'm taking you back,' was all he said, as he reached in and caught hold of her wrist and propelled her out of the taxi and down towards where his car was parked. 'Don't you ever walk out on me like that again,' he bit out at her furiously. 'No one turns their back on me, and certainly no woman!'

'Well, this one does!' Thea spat back at him, as he all but threw her into his car. 'But then I'm different, aren't I?' she added furiously, feeling the frustration well up inside her, he wasn't even going to allow her just that one last triumph.

She sat as far away from him as was possible in the space of the front seat, and gazed steadily out of the window, wishing the miles away to the time when she could get out of the car and slam the door behind her, and behind the whole of that wretched episode of her life.

As the car purred out of Pirates' Cove, Thea tried not to go over his brutal summing-up of what marriage meant to him, but the words seared through her brain as Sapphire's words had done. To think that Sapphire had been jealous of her, she thought pithily. She had credited him with more than he deserved, and had really thought that the marriage was for real, and how delighted she would have been when Marcus resumed their relationship again only a few months after the marriage.

Thinking of Sapphire reminded her that she would shortly be coming to the end of her performance at the hotel. 'You'd better hurry,' she said cuttingly to Marcus. 'Sapphire was furious when you let her down before. It's very hard to get taxis out there at this time of night.'

Marcus gave her a swift hard look before turning his attention to the road again. 'Don't push your luck, honey,' he growled ominously. 'At least Sapphire knows the score. You don't, but you're learning fast.'

There was simply no answer to that, Thea thought, furious at being classed with Sapphire as one of his women.

Soon the welcoming sight of Beach House came into view, and Marcus brought the big car to a sleek stop in front of the house.

Thea tried not to make a rush for the door, and as casually as she was able, she felt for the door catch, only to find Marcus's hand closing over hers, effectively preventing her from opening the door. 'How about a goodnight kiss?' he asked her mockingly.

'How about a jump in the lake!' retorted the incensed Thea, who was done with politeness, and her fury increased at his low chuckle.

'Change that to seven years,' he said in amusement, then released her hand from the catch. 'I'll pick you up at nine,' he said casually.

Thea got out of the car and whirled round to face him. Her wide eyes showing her disbelief that he could imagine for one moment that she—— 'I'm not going anywhere tomorrow,' she muttered through clenched teeth. 'So you're going to have a long wait!'

She hadn't believed anyone could move as fast as Marcus did then. One minute he was in the car favouring her with a sardonic look, the next moment he was beside her and pulling her into his arms with savage force. 'As I said, you're learning fast,' he said harshly, as he forced her head up by catching hold of the back of her head and making her submit to his kiss.

'I'm through playing footsie with you,' he said grimly as he released her after what seemed an age later. Thea had never been kissed like that before, and she was sure her lips must be swollen by such brutal treatment, because they hurt very much. 'And I don't know why the hell I bother!' he ground out. 'There's something about you that gets me, and the sooner I get it out of my system, the better. You're about as responsive as a stone wall,' he fumed at her. 'I take back all I said. You're right, honey—we'd never have made it. I need a woman, not a refrigerator!' and on this highly complimentary remark, he got back into his car and slammed the car door behind him with a force that must have jarred its hinges. The next moment the engine sprang into life, and with a screech of tires swept out of Thea's sight.

CHAPTER EIGHT

When Marcus had gone, Thea managed to find her door key. Her numbed fingers fumbled clumsily as she inserted it into the lock. Her eyes were dimmed by tears, not wholly of indignation, but with a deep sense of hurt.

Tomorrow, she told herself, as she climbed the stairs to her room, she would congratulate herself on successfully evading falling into the clutches of such a man. She would feel that much more able to cope with her future too, and one that quite definitely had nothing to do with Marcus Conan.

She wouldn't think about what happened that evening, even though her soft lips were now starting to sting from the rough treatment they had received from the brutal pressure of Marcus's lips.

'Is that you, Thea? Did you have a nice time?' Mrs Welling called, as Thea walked past her bedroom door.

'W—wonderful time, thank you, Mrs Welling,' Thea called back, hoping to be forgiven for the lie, and walked on quickly to her room in case Mrs Welling wanted to know anything else. There would be time enough to make up some plausible excuse as to why her latest gentleman friend, as Mrs Welling would have phrased it, had lost interest in her.

Thea slept well, she was too exhausted to keep awake, and sleep was a balm in itself. When she awoke the following morning to the same bright blue sky that she had awoken to since her arrival to the island, she still felt a sense of wonder that the sky would remain blue, and that the sun would shine all the day, for she had not been long enough on the island to take such things for granted. A sense of well-being flowed through her and she gave a luxurious stretch as she wondered what time it was.

There was a timid knock on her door a few minutes later, and Mrs Welling opened her door a fraction and called out, 'Are you awake, Thea? I've brought you a pot of tea.'

Receiving Thea's answer that she would love a cup of tea, she brought a tray in for her and placed it on the bedside table. 'You shouldn't spoil me like this,' Thea scolded her gently, as she sat up in bed. 'I ought to be bringing you your tea. You never have a lie-in.'

Mrs Welling smiled as she fussed about with arranging the cup and saucer ready to pour out the tea. 'I've never been able to lie-in,' she said. 'I've always got up early and I'm too old to change now,' she commented, as she poured Thea's tea out. 'You were back earlier than I thought you'd be,' she said conversationally, as she handed the tea to Thea.

Thea accepted the cup, and her eyes clouded over as she recalled the events of the evening. She also knew a pang of dismay, because it was obvious that Mrs Welling was longing to hear more about her distinguished visitor.

To stall for time, Thea took a sip of her tea while she considered the best way to handle the situation. Fortunately Marcus had not been all that attentive to her in Mrs Welling's presence but had concen-

trated his charm on the old lady. Her lips then met
the hot liquid and she winced in pain, then coughed
to cover her reaction and placed the tea down on
the bedside table again. 'I never could drink hot tea
first thing in the morning,' she said, smiling at Mrs
Welling, wondering how she could still smile. 'It
wasn't a date, you know,' she said carefully, to take
Mrs Welling's mind off her rejection of the tea.
'Well, at least not in the true sense of a date,' she
went on determinedly. 'He just wanted to know how
I was getting on. I did tell you that he felt responsible for me since my brother's death, didn't I?'
she added quickly. 'And it's very kind of him to
bother, isn't it?' she tacked on hurriedly.

Mrs Welling was clearly disappointed, and her
expression gave her away, but she rallied sufficiently
to say lamely, 'Well, as long as you had a nice time.'

Thea almost let out a great sigh of relief at this.
'Thank you, yes,' she replied, her voice sounding as
grateful as she felt at having got over that particular
hurdle. 'He gave me dinner, and then we sat and
talked for a while, then he brought me home,' she
offered, wondering if she dared risk taking another
sip of her tea.

'You know, seeing Mr Conan like that took me
back years,' said Mrs Welling, settling down on
Thea's bed. 'My sister used to work at their hotel—
oh, not the big complex he now owns, but the one
his parents owned.' She creased her brow in
thought, then brightened as she recalled the name of
the hotel. 'The Roxana, that's what it was called,'
she said, pleased with herself for remembering.
'Jenny—that was my sister—used to do the bedrooms—well, not only her, of course, it was a big

place in those days—but she was one of the bedroom staff, and she used to tell us little bits and
pieces about the family.'

She stared at the counterpane on which her hand
rested. 'Mr Conan's very like his father was at his
age,' she went on in a half-dreaming faraway voice.
'Just as good-looking, and he had a way with him
too. Wouldn't put up with fools. Very strong-
minded, you know, and that was half the trouble, I
think.'

Thea picked up her cup and tried an experi-
mental sip of the tea and found that it was now
possible to drink it. 'Trouble?' she asked, not really
wanting to continue the conversation; she had had
enough of the Conan family to last her a lifetime.

Mrs Welling nodded sagely. 'I'm afraid Mrs
Conan was strong-minded too,' she said, 'and the
rows they had were the talk of the island. She was
lovely, though,' she added wistfully, 'but very
spoilt. She was an actress, you know, and very successful, so naturally everyone was interested in her.'

She paused as she watched Thea finish her tea.
'Would you like another cup?' she asked kindly.

Thea's shake of the head was very decisive. 'No,
thank you,' she replied hastily. 'Did she go on with
her acting career after her marriage?' she asked,
now interested in what Mrs Welling was telling her.

'Oh, no!' Mrs Welling replied in a shocked voice.
'Mr Conan would not have allowed that, and really
that was what caused a lot of their trouble.' She
gave an emphatic nod, as if confirming her
thoughts. 'She missed all the glamour, I suppose,
and used to take her frustration out on him, but he
wasn't the type to take that without giving as good

as he got.' She gave a small shake of her head. 'It
couldn't have been a very happy atmosphere for a
child to grow up in,' she added slowly, then smiled
at Thea. 'Still, it doesn't appear to have done him
any harm, does it? I mean, a nicer gentleman you
couldn't wish to meet.'

Thea looked away hastily from Mrs Welling's
earnest expression. She had her own thoughts on
this, but decided not to disillusion her. 'Was M——
Mr Conan the only child?' she asked.

'Oh, yes,' Mrs Welling answered. 'The marriage
didn't last all that long. Well, it couldn't, could it?
Not when neither of them would give way, and they
must have got sick of the continual rows. I think it
only lasted long enough to let the child know who
was who, if you know what I mean, so that he could
get to know his parents.'

'Are they still alive?' Thea asked.

This brought another shake of Mrs Welling's grey
head. 'Mr Conan's father died five years ago, and
his mother, ' she frowned, 'some time before that, I
think. She'd left years before that to take up her
profession again.'

Thea stared unseeingly at the bedroom wall in
front of her. In a way it was an explanation of
Marcus's cynical view of life. It was no small
wonder that he didn't believe in marriage, but
surely he must have known of some happy mar-
riages, she thought sadly, they didn't all go sour.

'Well, I suppose I must let you get up,' Mrs Welling said, straightening herself up from the bed
slowly as a twinge of rheumatism caught her. 'I'd
better get the breakfasts going,' she added, 'although no one will be shouting yet awhile.'

Thea watched her walk slowly to the door, and before she had realised just what she was saying, she said quickly, 'Something did come up during our conversation last night. About getting a better job, my getting a better job,' she tacked on before her courage deserted her. 'He feels—that is, Mr Conan felt that I could do better for myself,' she lied, 'and although I'm quite happy as I am, I realise that he's right, so I thought I'd start looking around, if that's all right with you?' she asked hesitantly.

She was sure she had not imagined the look of relief on Mrs Welling's face before she replied in her usual blunt way. 'I told you that myself, didn't I? And I won't pretend that I wasn't worried about you. The job's only a stand-in position really, and I thought you would have started looking before now. No cause to worry about letting me down. I've decided to take Andy up on his offer, but I didn't want to say anything until I knew were settled. You go ahead now, and just as long as you promise to keep in touch with me in the future, I'll be well satisfied,' and with that she left to start the breakfasts.

Thea did not move out of the bed for quite some time after she had gone, but sat staring at the beams of sunlight playing on the floor of her bedroom. Her sudden decision to move on had surprised her. Without realising it, she had already made plans for her future, and knew exactly what she was going to do. She was going to get a very well paid job and save up for the fare back to the U.K. Beyond that she refused to think. She only knew that there was no future here for her, or on any sunlit tropical island. She simply didn't belong, and never would.

In years to come she would look back on this part of her life as an extended holiday, a trip into dreamland, maybe, for nothing was real there, even Marcus wouldn't seem real, but a figment of her imagination—only she wouldn't have imagined him as a ruthless character at all, it would have spoilt the dream, and Thea badly wanted to hang on to that dream. It was all she had, all she would ever have.

These miserable thoughts spurred her into action, and she jumped out of bed. She was not going into a decline over a man like that, he wasn't worth it. So, Marcus had had a hard upbringing, but so had others, and usually it worked the other way, with the memories of their childhood only serving to strengthen their resolve to provide their offspring with a happier and much more secure future, determined not to let them suffer the torment of the inevitable tug-of-war that followed a broken marriage.

Thea nodded grimly to herself as she towelled down after her shower. This was a fact that had to be faced, and no amount of whitewashing would change things. He had no excuse in her eyes, except for a selfish wish to avoid responsibility, and she had to remember that and not let sentimentality cloud her judgment.

After breakfast Thea went for a walk on the beach. The sun was warm on her bare arms as she followed the line of the bay. She wore a sleeveless cotton blouse over her sun top, in case she should want to do some sunbathing, and an old pair of brown corduroys over her shorts.

As she passed Timothy's boat, she wondered if he would appear that morning, and found herself wishing that he would, for she felt incredibly lonely. Although how she was going to explain Marcus's remark about her being his girl she didn't quite know, but she felt that given the time she could come up with something. She was turning out to be very adept at telling white lies, she thought musingly, as she scuffed her sandals in the golden sand beneath her feet.

Then she thought of the job that Marcus had been going to offer Timothy, and felt grateful that he would never know how near he had come to promotion—or what he would consider promotion, money-wise anyway. It would have been awful if he had been offered the job and then found out that his services were not required as Mr Big, as he had called Marcus, was no longer attracted to Thea John.

Her large grey eyes looked out over the bay, shimmering in the morning light. Silver-streaked ripples of water moved in eternal rhythm towards the shore. Her breath caught in her throat. She would miss all this, she thought. She would miss so many things, and in the midst of her heartbreak she would have to start all over again to make a new life for herself.

Why had her brother come to this island, and why had she come too? Why couldn't she have heard about the accident before she left England? What cruel stroke of fate had pitched her out of her secure complacency? She had been happy enough with the few friends she had back in her small home town. It might not have been a very exciting existence for her, but who wanted excitement, especially if you ended on the scrap heap of emotions as she had done.

She sat down on the warm sand and placed her arms around her knees, and resting her chin on her clasped hands gazed out to sea.

'You look like a sea waif,' said an amused voice behind her, making her start and swivel round quickly to meet Marcus's mocking eyes.

'I'm not in the mood for doubtful compliments,' Thea replied frostily, and as Marcus settled himself on the sand beside her she added waspishly, 'Will you please go away. We said all that was necessary yesterday.'

Marcus's green eyes narrowed at her tone, but he stayed where he was and followed Thea's gaze out to sea. 'Mrs Welling told me you were thinking of moving on,' he said conversationally.

'Mrs Welling talks too much,' Thea replied through clenched teeth.

'Why the sudden decision?' Marcus asked, ignoring her obvious reluctance to talk about it.

Thea gave an exasperated sigh. 'Why not?' she replied, purposely keeping her voice casual. 'I'm free and over twenty-one. I can please myself. This was only a stopgap until I found something better.'

Marcus turned to look at her and found that she was not looking at him, but at a seashell that she had picked up, and was examining it closely.

'It's a conch shell,' Marcus supplied helpfully. 'My offer's still open,' he added meaningfully.

Thea's hand clenched on the shell hard. 'I'm not that desperate!' she replied pithily.

The next moment she was lying flat on her back with Marcus's strong arms pinning her down on the golden sand, and she didn't care for the grim look on his face as he stared down at her. Then his large form completely blocked out the sunlight and he was kissing her forcefully.

Her small anguished moan as his hard lips pounded her already sore lips went unheeded at first, he was too intent on punishing her, but when he drew away from her, her tightly closed eyes and pained expression told its own story and his eyes went to her bruised lips. 'Hell, I'm sorry,' he said quietly, 'I guess most of the damage was done last night.' He gently kissed her sore lips before he moved away from her and allowed her to sit up again, the tears of disappointment and frustration teeming down her cheeks.

'Why can't you leave me alone!' Thea got out on a hopeless-sounding note.

'Think I haven't asked myself that question?' he shot back at her, handing her his large silk handkerchief. 'I came to apologise for last night, but look what happened. You rile me again, and I end up kissing the daylights out of you. I can't think of any other woman who invokes that response,' he ended grimly.

'That I would be so lucky!' Thea replied shakily, then took a deep breath and stared belligerently at him. 'What am I to do with you, Marcus Conan?' she sighed wearily. 'When are you going to stop plaguing me?'

'When you say you'll marry me, I guess,' he replied loftily.

'And end up a rich divorcee? No, thank you!' Thea replied steadily. 'I don't fancy that role at all.'

'It might not come to that,' he answered cautiously. 'We might decide to stay the course.'

She stared back at him. 'That's just the way you see it, isn't it? As a sort of an obstacle course, with all sorts of hidden snags.'

Marcus picked up the shell she had dropped when she had been thrown back on the sand. 'I guess so,' he replied grimly, 'and if you're honest you'll admit it. That dream world you're living in doesn't exist, sweet. Marriage is like a golf course, there's a few bunkers either side of the fairway.'

Thea's eyes left his and she gazed out to sea again. 'I know that,' she said quietly. 'That's the true test of love, don't you see? You don't love me. Oh, you want me, though I can't think why—I'm not glamorous like Sapphire, I'm a——' she searched desperately for the right definition. 'Oh, a country simpleton, if you like, and I'm not likely to change, neither are you. If I rile you it's because I don't happen to think the way you do. Tell me, what basis is that for marriage?' She shook her head bewilderedly, making the sun-rays catch the red lights in her hair and framing her small face like a fiery torch. 'You of all people must know what sort of a marriage that will be.'

Marcus's eyes left the seashell and he gave her a hard searching stare. 'You're right, Mrs Welling does talk too much!' he commented savagely.

Thea looked away quickly. 'I didn't ask her about you,' she said in a low voice. 'She brought me some tea in this morning, and stayed for a chat. If you want to know,' she added quietly, 'she thinks you're the tops, in spite of what she called an earlier handicap.'

Marcus's profile seemed to be made out of granite as he stared out to sea again. 'So that's the excuse you're giving me, is it?' he asked her harshly. 'Well, I'm sorry, honey, but you're way off course. Oh, I guess if I hadn't been in the business I'm in, I might have had some call to turn sour, but that's only a small part of it. Sure, they rowed, but underneath it all they were pretty fond of each other, and if my mother hadn't died in an automobile accident I'm sure they'd have got together again.'

He was silent for a few seconds before he said: 'In my business you see it all. The sweet loving wife, who the minute her husband's back's turned is giving you the eye, it's all a game to them, but it's sure hell for the poor devil of a husband who happens to be sucker enough to love his wife.'

Thea winced at his hard tone. If he wasn't quite so handsome or so rich, he wouldn't have had such experiences, she thought sadly, and marvelled again over the fact that he wanted to marry her. It was flattering, of course, especially if he expected the same of her as he did of other women. 'I see,' she said carefully. 'Well, at least I shall know what's expected of me, should I marry you.'

Marcus's head swivelled round sharply at this, and he glared at her. 'You try it, my girl, that's all,' he said savagely. 'Two-time me just once, and you'll never do it again.'

Thea, meeting those cold hard eyes of his, felt a shiver run down her spine. He meant it, she was in no doubt of that. Heaven help the girl he did fall in love with, she thought, he'd never let her out of his sight.

Above everything else, this proved to Thea that whatever attraction she held for Marcus, it was purely physical. He hadn't bothered to look her up for a

fortnight after she had walked out on him. He had
said himself that he didn't know why he bothered.
He had also called her a refrigerator! Thea's hands
gathered up some of the fine sand and she let it
slowly run through her fingers. Was that the attraction? she wondered. He wouldn't have met many
refrigerated women either, she mused ironically; the
accent would definitely be on the hothouse variety!

In a way, he was like a small boy who had been
denied something that he had wanted, and he
wasn't used to such treatment. Everything had been
there for the asking, he had only to reach out and
take it, and when he tired of the toy, throw it away.

Her soft lips, still tingling from their rough treatment, trembled. She wasn't going to become one of
his toys, he would have to look elsewhere for his
amusement, and she hated him for making her fall
in love with him. 'You remind me of a small boy,'
she said scathingly, wanting to hurt him as much as
she was hurting inside. 'You just think you can take
what you like, regardless of the consequences.
You've never been denied anything, have you?
That's really why you're chasing me. Why don't you
admit it? I'm not your type, and I hope I never shall
be,' she declared fervently. 'I think I can see Timothy,' she added in a rush, as she began to scramble
up from the sand, 'so if you don't mind, I'll keep
that belated date with him.'

For the second time that morning Thea found
herself flat on the sand again, and she glared up at
Marcus, who looked as furious as she felt. 'I told you
once before that I don't like my women walking out
on me,' he growled ominously, 'and I've already
planned our day. I don't know what you've got

against that man,' he added in grim amusement, 'you're sure trying to make life tough for him. Do him a favour and stay away from him,' he advised her in a soft but deadly voice.

'And I've told you that I'm not one of your women!' Thea spat back at him, wriggling her arms to free them from his steely hold, but all in vain.

'I think your Timothy can see us from where he is now,' he commented softly, releasing his hold from her and letting her sit up. 'Attempt to join him, and you'll find that little boy you referred to just now has suddenly grown up. It would be a shame to put you through more kisses,' he added silkily, his eyes on her lips.

Thea gave a slight shudder at the very thought. It would be bad enough being on the receiving end, without the thought of Timothy witnessing such an action.

They watched the boat sail past them on its way out to the bay and Timothy waved to them before he headed the boat out to sea. Beside her, Marcus lifted his hand in a silent salute, and Thea waved a tentative hand in his direction, hoping that Marcus would not object to this small gesture on her part, for she knew he was still seething inwardly from her remarks and would dearly love to punish her.

'As for not denying myself anything,' he said in a low voice, his eyes on the boat that was gradually getting smaller in the distance, 'I guess you're right there, and as for taking what I wanted,' his eyes suddenly turned to her wary ones, 'I've never had to go that far, but I don't say I wouldn't if it was important enough to me. You can draw your own conclusions on that,' he added harshly. 'I'd say I was the one who had grown up, and you hadn't. You're going to have to lose those rose-tinted spectacles you're hiding behind.'

Thea looked away from his compelling eyes and stared down at her hands. Her slim fingers prodded the soft sand. If she had been wearing rose-tinted spectacles, she had lost them the previous evening when she had gained an insight into his world.

Marcus glanced at his watch and then got to his feet, and before Thea knew his intention he had hauled her to her feet, too. 'We've a lunch appointment,' he said grandly.

Thea knew a helpless sensation. She would be wasting her time if she tried to get out of it. Her depressed glance went to her old corduroys and back to the watching Marcus.

'You'll do fine,' he told her with a grin. 'You can sunbathe on the terrace after lunch.'

Thea blinked. How had he known that she wore her sun-suit underneath?

He gave her a sardonic smile and placed a lean forefinger on her waist. Following his glance, Thea saw that the bright blue band of her shorts had edged above her corduroys. 'There's not much I miss, where you're concerned,' he said loftily, making her want to hit out at him.

'I ought to tell Mrs Welling that I won't be in for lunch,' Thea said crossly, letting him know that there were other people in the world, even though they did not figure in his.

'No need,' Marcus replied blandly, as he steered her away from the house and towards his car parked a little to the right of the house. 'I outlined our plans for the day. I also promised not to keep you out too late,' he gave a grin at Thea's indignant glance at him. 'Unless I'm much mistaken, she's the type who doesn't settle down until their chicks have come home to roost.'

There was nothing Thea could say to this, but she was surprised that Marcus had taken the trouble to keep Mrs Welling in the picture, and more so by his thoughtful assurance of not keeping her out too late.

As she got into the car, she wondered if she had misjudged him; it appeared that he did have some good points after all.

'We're having lunch with Mr and Mrs Smythe,' he told her as he started the car and steered it skilfully off the bumpy parking section and on to the road. 'I don't know if you'll remember meeting John. He's got a chain of hotels in Florida. I was there last week for a confab with him,' he offered casually. 'He's got his eye on developing this end of the island, something on the lines of Pirates' Cove,' he went on, 'and he's trying to talk me into joining the venture.'

Thea glanced back at Marcus and wondered what she was supposed to say to that. It was none of her business, but she had to say something. 'And will you?' she asked, more for politeness' sake than for interest.

Marcus shrugged. 'I feel I've got enough on my plate,' he said slowly. 'I'll probably offer financial backing, but that's as far as I'll go. John's the nicest guy I know. His wife is a different proposition,' he added meaningfully.

Thea had been gazing out at the passing scenery of clumps of palm trees that went high into the blue haze of the sky, but at this she looked quickly at

Marcus. 'You don't like his wife?' she asked, interested this time, although she had a pretty good idea of what was coming next.

'She's a fool!' he said curtly. 'She was a receptionist in one of his hotels, although she wouldn't thank you for reminding her of that now. So he whisks her out of her downtown apartment and marries her. He's crazy about her, so crazy that he turns a blind eye to her little drawbacks such as giving the come-on sign to any presentable male within distance. One day she's going to go just that bit too far. There's a limit to what a man will put up with, even a nice guy like John. One day he's going to wake up and really look at her and see her for what she is.'

Thea studied Marcus's hard features, and felt depression seeping over her. So that was why he had dragged her off to lunch. He needed help, and the homely-looking Thea John was supposed to provide that help, particularly as they had been engaged —She blinked suddenly as a thought occurred to her. 'When did I meet this John?' she asked casually.

'The night before we got engaged,' Marcus replied, just as casually.

When she was still starry-eyed, Thea thought miserably, and wondered what the said John would think of their new relationship. 'Does he know that we got engaged?' she asked carefully.

Marcus threw her a sardonic look. 'Sure he knows,' he answered softly. 'I guess he wants to congratulate you.'

Thea drew in a deep breath. 'So you didn't tell him it was off. That wasn't very kind of you,' she said indignantly. 'He's going to feel a bit foolish now, isn't he?'

'I had my reasons for not enlightening him,' Marcus replied with the autocratic note back in his voice, 'and I want it left like that.' He gave her a hard quick assessing look. 'I said you owed me, didn't I?' he said meaningfully.

Thea stared back at him. 'When exactly will you consider the debt paid?' she demanded furiously. 'I only want some idea of how often I'm going to be dragged out on mercy missions,' and her fury increased as he gave a deep chuckle. 'I might be slow, but I've got the picture,' she went on acidly. 'You're using me, aren't you, to fend off this woman. If he does decide to go ahead with that hotel idea, then they'll be around a long time,' she fumed. 'I advise you to look around for another fiancée. I don't plan to be around that long!'

Marcus shot her another of those quick assessing looks of his. 'Careful, honey,' he warned softly. 'I could stop the car and make you a little better disposed towards things. I don't give a damn about Moira Smythe, and if you think I'm looking for a skirt to hide behind, then you don't know me very well. I've had plenty of practice in handling such women. I wouldn't have got far in my business if I hadn't learned fast. If you want to put it down to anything, try the pride aspect. It isn't every day a man gets engaged and is jilted the next,' he added, now as furious as Thea had been.

Thea looked away from his blazing eyes and down at her hands now twisted in her lap. She swallowed hard. He couldn't have chosen a better explanation to make her feel as mean as she felt then.

It wasn't her fault that she had been naïve and hadn't seen behind Marcus's proposal, but had accepted it without question. 'That wasn't very kind of you,' she said quietly, her eyes still on her hands. 'You know why I backed out.'

'And now you know my thoughts on the matter,' Marcus replied harshly. 'I guess you were right, though—the way things are shaping up we'd need a referee, not a best man!'

Thea's nails dug into her soft palms. It was going to be a wonderful luncheon party, she thought miserably, and if John Smythe still thought they were in love with each other it wouldn't only be his wife's shortcomings that he was blind to!

CHAPTER NINE

JOHN and Moira Smythe were waiting for them on the hotel terrace when they arrived at Pirates' Cove. Thea had a vague recollection of meeting John Smythe, who was thirtyish, and rather plump, and had seemed a nice uncomplicated type of man.

His wife, a woman in her late twenties, Thea judged, in spite of the bright golden curls dexterously arranged around her small but drawn-looking features, that suggested that she had a weight problem and had overdone the dieting, gave the impression that she was a vague helpless female who needed a strong helping hand to help her over the pitfalls of life, preferably male. Her warm overeffusive greeting to Thea was accepted by her with inward reservations, and Thea kept a watching eye on her during lunch.

As they sat down at the table in the alcove, already prepared for lunch, Thea was very conscious of her cotton blouse and corduroys, and felt that she must have given the impression that she had been hauled out of a fishing trip, or some other activity that did not require dressing-up. Moira Smythe's gorgeous silk peacock blue dress that clung to her slim figure emphasised her discomfiture and she felt obliged to apologise for her appearance.

This apparently annoyed Marcus, who obviously did not like her apologising for anything, and she had hardly finished before he added, 'We had a morning on the beach, and I'm afraid I overlooked the time.' He gave Thea a possessive look. 'I didn't allow her time to change,' he added, in a manner that implied that he was boss of the outfit, and Thea felt her cheeks grow warm as she felt Moira's curious eyes on her.

It was true, every bit of it, Thea thought furiously. She had not been allowed any leeway. She would never be allowed any, where he was concerned, and in spite of the envious looks she was getting from the woman sitting opposite her, Thea found no consolation in this state of affairs.

John Smythe gave a hearty chuckle and clapped Marcus on the shoulder. 'That's the way, old man,' he said heartily. 'Start as you mean to go on.' He gave Thea a wide grin. 'It's a case of humouring the brute, Thea, but I guess you've already found that out for yourself, eh?'

His enjoyment of the situation subsided quickly as he met his wife's cold eyes, and Thea felt immensely sorry for him. There had been no love or understanding in that look, only open boredom from the woman he loved.

'Oh, I've soft-pedalled with her so far,' Marcus replied softly, breaking into Thea's musings, 'but she's learning fast, aren't you darling?' he taunted mockingly.

Thea's eyes did not speak of love either as they met his, and she wondered what he would do if she said what she thought of his tactics. She didn't have to wonder for long, the look in his eyes said all that was necessary, and she hastily applied herself to the lunch now being served.

When they reached the coffee stage, the talk had

turned to less embarrassing matters, and the men began to discuss business.

'I took a look around yesterday,' said John, lighting up a cigar. 'There's an old place there on the hill—some sort of rooming-house, I guess. It's a bit of an eyesore, though, and I could use that land. I'll have to see what can be done about it,' he ruminated.

Thea looked up then, remembering what Marcus had said about the plan to develop that part of the island. 'Beach House?' she asked.

'That was its name, or something like it,' he replied in a surprised way. 'You know it, do you? Wouldn't happen to know who owns it, would you?' he queried.

Thea's eyes went to Marcus as she replied slowly, 'As a matter of fact, yes. I live there. The owner is Mrs Welling—but she won't sell out,' she added firmly.

John Smythe shrugged. 'Everyone's got a price,' he said with a grin. 'It's worth making the approach, anyway.'

Marcus looked at Thea. 'She told me she was thinking of joining her nephew. Said the business was getting a bit too much for her to handle,' he said quietly.

Thea nodded her confirmation of this. 'But she's not selling up,' she said firmly. 'She wants to keep it as a boarding house and put a manager in. Those boarders have been with her for a long time.'

'Well, if it's just a question of finding them other accommodation, I guess there's no problem there. It will be worth letting off a few flats to clear the area,' said John heartily.

'At a price that they can afford?' Thea queried with an ironic note in her voice. 'And what if they don't want to move? They look on Beach House as their home,' she added indignantly.

John gave Marcus a quick, amused look. 'Say, you got a philanthropist there?' he queried lightly.

Marcus reached over and caught Thea's slim waist and pulled her towards him. 'I'm not sure,' he replied grandly, 'but whatever she is, I'm hanging on to her.'

Thea could feel his strong fingers spanning her waist, touching the bare flesh in the gap between her blouse and corduroys, and felt her knees go weak. She wanted to pull away from him, but knew better than to give way to this fear of his proximity.

'Must we talk business?' Moira cut in impatiently, as if unable to bear the sight of someone receiving such lover-like attention from a man she had had her sights on for a long time. She had been perfectly patient until then, Thea mused silently, quite content to let the men talk.

John gave his wife a surprised look. 'We came over to discuss business, honey-plum—I told you that. Slip down to the beach and get some sun bathing in if you're bored,' he suggested.

'By myself?' she replied pettishly. 'No, thank you!' She gave Thea an almost calculating look. 'Unless you want to join me?' she asked her hopefully.

Thea was torn between getting out of Marcus's deceptively loving hold on her waist, yet wanting to hear what John Smythe decided to do about Beach House in order to warn Mrs Welling of his plans.

She might have known that Marcus would settle the matter. 'Use the end of the terrace,' he suggested. 'It's not so crowded as the beach. We'll join you later for tea.'

As Thea settled herself down on one of the lounge chairs left out on Marcus's private sector of the terrace, and waited while Moira went back into the hotel to change into her sunsuit, she thought about Marcus's marked change of tactics where she was concerned. She particularly recalled his remark of 'soft-pedalling', as he had put it, with her until now. If that was soft-pedalling, Thea hated to think what lay in store for her from now on. She was woman enough to feel a thrill of expectation towards the future, but sensible enough not to let these feelings rule her head.

He could have been putting on an act for the Smythes, but somehow Thea didn't think so. It wasn't in character, and that left the other alternative. He was intent on punishing her for refusing to play his game. She had hurt his pride, he had admitted it, and that couldn't have been easy for him either.

From where she lay on the upper terrace, she could see the beach below, and now and again would hear snatches of children's laughter. The sound seemed to sear through her heightened senses. She dearly loved Marcus, she would always love him, but could she deny herself children? It was his children she wanted, no one else's. Could she accept marriage with a man who didn't love her, and would one day throw her aside when her attraction for him ended?

Her eyes narrowed as she envisaged such a future. She would wake each morning and wonder if this was the day when Marcus would ask her to get out of his life, and she would have to face up to years of loneliness and yearning for a man who no longer cared for her.

She shook her head blindly. She must ignore the feelings his touch invoked in her. The future was all that mattered, and what would be in store for her should she let her heart rule her head. She must leave this place, she thought wildly, or she would be lost. What chance did she stand against a man like that? All the odds were in his favour, and he knew it, she thought frantically.

Had Moira not arrived at that precise time, Thea would have grabbed her corduroys and blouse and made a run for it while Marcus was otherwise engaged.

'Correct me if I'm wrong,' Moira murmured as she settled herself down on a lounger beside Thea, 'but I have a feeling that you're not so keen on that gorgeous hunk of man as you're supposed to be.'

Thea's eyes widened at this very astute guess on Moira's part, and as she sought for a plausible explanation for her unloverlike response to Marcus, she absently noticed the bright green bikini that she wore, and the wisp of material at the top giving maximum leeway for an all-over tan. 'I suppose I'm a bit reserved,' she replied cautiously, and hastily looked away from Moira's very knowing eyes.

Moira gave a sigh, and laid her head down on the chair back, 'I've heard that Englishmen are cold,' she said, with a touch of dry humour in her voice. 'I didn't know that went for the women as well.'

There was a few moments' silence after this, and Thea closed her eyes and let the warmth of the sun seep through her, hoping that Moira would choose another subject if she was inclined to talk, but she found that the wish was not to be fulfilled.

'You want to watch it,' Moira went on thought-fully. 'His type doesn't play around, and there's plenty who'd grab at the chance of making his interest permanent.'

Sapphire, for instance, Thea thought miserably, and goodness knows how many more—Moira herself, if it came to that, she thought, remembering the way she had hardly taken her eyes off him during lunch. If only to show that she wasn't as slow as Moira apparently thought she was, Thea remarked dryly, 'You mean Sapphire, I suppose?'

Moira lifted her head in a surprised action and stared at her. 'I shouldn't worry about Sapphire,' she said caustically, then relaxed back to her former position. 'She's done very well for herself out of the Conan family. She was lucky Marcus adhered to his father's wishes and looked out for her future. She's a fool if she thinks it goes any further than that, and no amount of wishful thinking will change things.'

Thea's eyes jerked open, and she sat bolt upright and stared at Moira, who lay with her eyes closed and her face turned towards the sun. 'Was Sapphire——' She swallowed, and took a deep breath, but could not go on; in any case there was no need.

Moira gave a smile that reminded Thea of a cat, a Cheshire cat, contemplating a large bowl of cream. 'His father's mistress? Yes,' she supplied happily, wriggling herself into a more comfortable position and clearly enjoying herself, 'it's not something that Marcus would want broadcast around the island though, and most people thought that she was his property. Went for you, did she?' she asked in amusement.

Thea was still trying to come to terms with this startling revelation from the past. She recalled Pauline's remarks about Sapphire and how she had been around for a long time. Five years was a long time, and it had been that length of time since his father had died. A lot could happen in that time, she thought dully. She couldn't see any man passing up the opportunity of getting a little better acquainted with such a sultry beauty as Sapphire, particularly if they were given the green light, not even Marcus. 'Five years is a long time,' she half-muttered to herself, speaking her thoughts aloud.

'Since Mr Conan's death?' Moira queried, beaming in accurately on Thea's thoughts. 'Five—ten years. It wouldn't make any difference to Marcus. He's not the man to take anyone's leavings, and certainly not his father's. Even if he'd been tempted— and he wasn't,' she added with an air of satisfaction in her voice. 'Oh, she's got the figure, but the rest is a façade. To give her her due, she's never given up. Marcus tolerates her, but that's as far as it goes.'

Thea slowly lay back and closed her eyes. She badly wanted to be alone to be able to absorb all that she had heard, but most of all she wanted Marcus near her. To tell him how much she had misjudged him, and how much she loved him.

This euphoric feeling did not last long, however, and was soon replaced by the same old nagging doubts. Nothing really had changed. Marcus still had the same views on marriage, and more important than this was the bare fact that he didn't love her. A child's laugh floated up to her from the beach below and Thea winced. When he did fall in love he would want children, it was a natural conclusion of a truly happy marriage.

'You don't know how lucky you are,' Moira went on, unaware of the turbulent thoughts going through Thea's mind. 'Now if I were lucky enough to catch the eye of a man like that, I'd be on cloud nine. I wouldn't walk, I'd float!' she added dreamily. Then her voice changed to a pettish tone. 'But look what I've got. Can you imagine anyone less romantic-looking than my husband?' she demanded irritably.

'Looks don't always count,' Thea replied carefully. 'I like John, and it's obvious that he loves his wife,' she reminded her.

'Oh, sure,' Moira replied in a bored tone, 'but looks go a long way to sweeten the medicine.'

Thea felt a dark depression settle over her. She didn't love her husband at all, and she was beginning to understand Marcus's attitude towards marriage. 'Looking forward to being a rich divorcee?' she asked the scowling Moira as she pondered on her miserable lot in life.

This comment produced an amazing reaction from Moira, who sat bolt upright, much as Thea had done earlier, and glared at Thea. 'Who said anything about divorce?' she demanded, then simmered down as she met Thea's startled expression. 'Okay,' she said slowly, her eyes on her hands with her brightly painted nails, 'so I let off steam now and again, but I'm no fool. I know where I'm better off. I'm not aiming to land up as a black widow.' She met Thea's puzzled look. 'That's what they're called,' she explained. 'They pretend they're having a whale of a time, but the only parties they go to are the ones they throw themselves. They'd be after my

John like a cloud of locusts if given the chance.' She broke off suddenly as if a thought had just occurred to her. 'Say, there's nothing been said, has there?' she asked Thea, lines of anxiety now plainly visible on her smooth creamed forehead, then took a deep breath. 'Oh, forget it, honey,' she said casually, and lay back on the lounger again, but the anxiety was still in her eyes, Thea noticed, in spite of her added, 'John's okay. I make sure of that.'

Thea was certain that she had inadvertently given Moira a deep shock, even though she had tried to hide this fact from her. 'Only you've no children, have you?' she asked her after a few seconds' silence. 'I'm sorry, I don't mean to probe,' she went on, 'but John strikes me as a family man. Didn't he want any children?' she asked innocently.

Moira half-turned towards her, and Thea could see she was surprised at the question, and now gave it some deep thought. 'I guess he left the choice up to me,' she said slowly, and her light blue eyes narrowed in thought. 'It might be an idea at that,' she commented quietly, then turned over on her stomach exposing a well-oiled back towards the sun. 'Thanks, honey,' she murmured.

That was all she said, but Thea knew what she meant, and felt a surge of accomplishment. John Smythe was in for a very pleasant shock in the near future, unless she had miscalculated the matter, but Thea was sure she hadn't. She thought of John's remark about her being a philanthropist—perhaps she was, she thought, as she settled down to sunbathe again. If only she could sort her own problems out to a happy conclusion!

Moira's remarks on divorce confirmed Thea's

own thinking. It was certainly not a state of existence to make one's goal, although Marcus had
seemed to think that that was the prime motive of
marriage for most women, with a fat settlement following and freedom to do as one wished for the rest
of time. He ought to have heard Moira's bald summing-up on the subject, Thea thought sadly, but he
would only see what he wanted to see.

The Smythes left in the early evening, in an
atmosphere of congeniality, with Moira paying particular attention to her rather mystified but very
satisfied husband.

To Thea's surprise Marcus took her back to
Beach House shortly after they left, saying that he
had some paper work to get through that evening,
as he had promised to let John have some figures by
midday the following day.

Although relieved, Thea wondered if he had another engagement. She had served her purpose, she
thought distractedly as she gazed out of the car
window as they left Pirates' Cove. It was already
beginning, she thought; he couldn't wait to get rid
of her. Was he meeting Sapphire? she wondered.
She had so wanted to believe what Moira had told
her about his relationship with Sapphire, but there
was no getting away from the fact that he had called
to pick her up from the hotel that evening, and Sapphire had expected him to do so the following evening. Giving her a helping hand with her career was
one thing, but he hadn't had to dance attendance
on her afterwards, not unless——

Thea swallowed hard. This kind of thinking was
getting her nowhere, and to take her mind off this
dangerous line of reasoning she asked, 'What did

John decide to do about Beach House?' She ought to
have asked before, she thought, but she had been so
immersed in her own complicated world.

Marcus had been noticeably quiet during the
drive, but he now shot her a quick look before he
answered almost absentmindedly, 'What he said he
would do about it,' in the tone of voice that showed
that he wasn't interested in such a mundane subject.

Thea gave an abrupt nod at this. It was clear that
he was not going to discuss the matter further, and
she felt he had shut her out of his thoughts, even
though he must have known that she was interested.
So that was that, she told herself stoutly. He would
probably say something on the lines of 'be seeing
you,' after he dropped her off at Beach House. That
was what they all said, she thought dully, and could
almost hear him saying it.

When the car drew up in front of the house, Thea
felt she could hardly look at Marcus, but managed
to say brightly as she got out of the car, not waiting
for him to alight, 'Well, thanks for the day out,' and
started to walk quickly towards the door, and her
step faltered slightly as he called out, 'Be seeing
you.'

Thea did not turn round but kept on walking,
and waved what she hoped was an airy answer. By
the time she had opened the door the car had gone.

It was no use hoping that Mrs Welling had gone
to bed, it was much too early, and Thea braved
herself for an evening's gossip with the old lady, although she would much rather have gone straight to
her room and allowed herself the luxury of a few
tears.

To Mrs Welling's kind enquiry of would she like

anything to eat, Thea replied that she had had what might be called a high tea and wouldn't require anything else. She could tell by the old lady's manner that she was pleased to see her, for she had got used to Thea's company each evening, and Thea wondered how she would manage when she moved out to the flat, as her nephew would be on the sea cruises most of the time. As yet Thea did not know what part of Charlotte Amalie the flat was in, but she hoped it was within striking distance of the hotel that her brother managed, so she would have some company either from her brother or from Pauline.

When they had settled down in the lounge, Thea broached the subject of John Smythe's proposals for that section of the island. 'He's got his eye on Beach House,' she said, closely watching Mrs Welling's reaction to the news.

'No harm in that,' Mrs Welling replied comfortably. 'That's as far as he'll get. I'm not selling up,' she added firmly.

'That's what I told him,' said Thea.

'Good for you, then,' replied Mrs Welling in a satisfied voice. 'What did he say to that?' she asked curiously.

Thea shrugged. 'Seemed to think that if the offer was high enough you'd have second thoughts,' she said dryly.

Her companion smiled and shook her head. 'There's things money can't buy,' she commented quietly, 'and this is one of them. What would I do with a lot of money at my age? It's an interest I need, and it's what I'll have. I can't see myself sitting in that flat of Andy's all day with practically nothing to do. That's not for me. I'm not an idler.'

'Where is the flat?' Thea asked quickly, having a nasty feeling that her news might well have made her change her mind about leaving Beach House, and neither Andy nor Pauline would thank her for that; they had the old lady's welfare at heart, as had Thea.

'It's very near Joseph's hotel. Andy didn't want me stranded on my own. I don't intend to make a nuisance of myself to either him or Pauline, but it will be nice to have them near,' Mrs Welling answered, adding hastily, 'I hope you will keep in touch too, dear, after you get settled.'

As Thea gave her word on this she wondered when that would be. There was the question of finding herself another job to start with, and that only to save up for her return fare back to the U.K., but she said nothing of this to Mrs Welling, who now began to ply her with questions about the new venture.

'Did he actually say it was this part of the beach he was interested in?' she queried. 'Only there's a much better spot further up, with a little cove. It's used by a few locals who want to avoid the crowds, but there's no amenities there,' she went on thoughtfully. 'I would have thought that would have been a better proposition for him.'

Thea was now very tired and wanted to make her escape, but her voice showed none of this. 'I think it's early days yet,' she answered carefully. 'I've a feeling he's just casting around for ideas. You'll have to mention this place to him when he waves his wallet at you,' she commented smilingly. 'Now, would you mind if I went to bed?' she asked.

When Thea got to her room she did not immediately prepare herself for bed but sat on the window ledge gazing out across the bay.

Marcus's airy 'Be seeing you,' mocked her in her silent reverie. What a strange, unpredictable man he was! Bullying her and demanding her company, regardless of her wishes in the matter, and then depositing her at the front door early in the evening, but too late for her to make alternative arrangements for an evening out—not that she had anywhere else to go, but she might have had, she thought sadly.

Now that he had admitted that she had hurt his pride, Thea was able to understand his reasoning, but could gain little consolation from this. If only she could be certain that he had decided that she wasn't worth bothering about and would leave her in peace from now on, but she could be sure of nothing where he was concerned. Her hands clenched in her lap. She had to go. The island was too small. Her original idea of keeping out of his way was just not going to work; he would see to that. Her smooth brow creased in thought. Was that what he wanted? she wondered. He hadn't liked her taking the kiosk job, and that was pride, too. No matter where she went on the island, her former connection with Marcus was bound to come out sooner or later, and it wouldn't have been long before Timothy found out about it either.

She gave a deep sigh. If it had been anyone else but 'Mr Big', as Timothy had called him, it wouldn't have mattered one little bit. Lots of people got engaged and broke it off later—not perhaps the very next day, she thought sadly, as she recalled Marcus's bitter comment on this earlier, but it did

happen and was not unheard of. Marcus had not
seen it that way, though, and had accused her of
playing with him. No wonder he had been so savage
with her when she had attempted to join Timothy!
She put a tentative hand up to her lips and gave a
slight sigh. The misty look in her eyes was not at all
due to Timothy, but had a much deeper cause. It
was bad enough knowing that the man you loved did
not return that love, but it was worse still when you
knew that his only motivation was a kind of revenge
that would eventually turn to hate, and it was just
possible that that process had already begun, she
thought, as she recalled that he had barely spoken to
her on the journey back from Pirates' Cove. She
might have been a waxed effigy for all the notice he
had taken of her.

   Thea got up wearily from the window sill. There
was only one way out, and that was right out. This
was no time for half measures, or for hoping things
would alter. She had to get a better paid job, and
save like mad, she told herself as she undressed. First
thing in the morning she would collect all the papers
and find out if there was an employment agency in
the town. Mrs Welling would help her there, she
told herself stoutly, and if the worst came to the
worst, then she would ask for her old job back at the
hotel. Marcus had said it was still vacant, and Sapphire or no Sapphire, Thea would swallow her pride
and go back. Pride was something she couldn't
afford now, and the job was a well paid one.

   By the time she had had her shower and got into
bed, she had made her mind up. It was the thought
of Pauline that had decided her. She had sorely
missed her gay chatter and her company during her

off-duty periods. Sapphire would be half-way through her three-month stint at the hotel, and as Pauline had said, she was only there for two nights of the week.

Thea put out her bedside light and laid her head down on the pillows. In a strange way she felt relieved, as if it was all over, and all she had to worry about now was getting enough money together for her fare back home to England. Pauline would understand her reasoning, and although she might try and talk her out of leaving the island, she was sensible enough to see things from her point of view, she thought drowsily as she drifted off to sleep.

The following morning, however, things did not seem quite so cut and dried. It was all very well taking Marcus at his word and assuming that she could just walk into the hotel and claim her job back. Someone must have done her work during the few weeks that she had been away, and whoever it was, they would not relish being moved on, but that was precisely what would happen, Thea was certain. Pauline's Uncle Joseph was not likely to risk getting at loggerheads with one of the hotel directors, particularly if it was Marcus Conan.

Thea was in very low spirits later that morning as she went down to open the kiosk. She didn't want to move on, and she dreaded the inevitable drudge round the town looking for work, and the ensuing explanation as to why she was in St Thomas and so far from her homeland, and worse still, that she only wanted temporary work at the highest possible pay to enable her to get back home. She swallowed. They would class her as a drifter, and she couldn't blame them. Very probably they would show her the door before she had finished talking at the interview.

'Morning, missy, lovely day!' called a cheerful voice as Thea inserted the key into the door of the kiosk, and a pair of large black hands relieved her of her tray of rolls that she had been balancing under one arm as she opened the door.

She had been so preoccupied with her miserable musings that she had not seen Sam rise from his usual position at the side of the kiosk at her approach. Her startled stare met the merry brown eyes of Sam. 'Hello,' she said, sounding as surprised as she felt at his appearance, then her soft lips firmed. 'You're still on guard duty, then?' she queried with a hint of sarcasm in her voice, and then felt instantly contrite, and added hastily, 'I missed you on Saturday.'

For this little act of friendship on her part she was rewarded by a huge grin from Sam as he placed the tray on the counter. 'Boss said, okay, he take over,' he replied in his soft island accent.

Boss took over right enough, Thea thought sourly as she started to arrange the rolls ready for sale, for she could see her first customers already approaching.

Sam's continued presence at the kiosk puzzled her until she realised that Marcus would hardly have had time to call him off the job. So convinced was she that he had lost interest in her, and that she could now take a job as a stevedore without him batting an eyelid.

When the first rush of customers had passed, Thea leant on the counter with her face cupped in her hands and gazed out over the brilliant blue bay, watching the sailing boats drifting up and down the bay, their different coloured sails adding to the panorama of colour around her. She would remember all this, she thought, when she got back to England, and then had to blink quickly to remove the wetness gathering in her eyes.

It was all so unfair. Losing Michael had been bad enough without losing her heart to a man like Marcus Conan. Whatever happened in the future, she would never be whole again. Part of her would always be here, and the other part yearning to join it. In the years to come she would ask herself why she hadn't married Marcus. Why she hadn't snatched at happiness while she had the chance. The old saying of 'better to have loved and lost than never to have loved at all' came to mind, and she swallowed hard. She just couldn't take the 'lost' bit of that old saying. One might just as well say, let's live for today and forget tomorrow, but tomorrow would loom forever on her horizon like a threatening cloud that heralds a storm, and the thought of the bleak future ahead of her would eclipse any chance of happiness.

It was a pity that she couldn't go back to Bay View, she thought sadly, for she was certain that Marcus was still seeing Sapphire, and it would have done her good to actually witness him collecting her from the hotel again. As Pauline had said, old habits die hard, and Thea suspected that Moira's interpretation of his relationship with Sapphire was the result of sheer pique on her part, unable to accept that someone else had succeeded where she had failed. She didn't know how long Moira had been married to John, but one thing was certain, and that was that she had hung out the welcome sign in Marcus's direction on more than one occasion, hence his unwillingness to entertain them on his own.

It was getting near to closing time when Timothy suddenly appeared at the kiosk, and Thea, who was busy clearing up and getting ready to cash up the day's takings, drew in a swift inward breath of dismay as she wondered how she was going to explain her earlier duplicity. She owed him an apology, and somehow she had to try and convince him that she hadn't meant to deceive him—and it was going to be so difficult, she thought miserably.

'Hi, there!' said Timothy, before Thea could begin her explanation. 'I couldn't move on without saying a big thank-you to my fairy godmother, could I?' he grinned. 'Although I'll see you around some time, I guess,' he added, with a wink at the astounded Thea, and then looked over to his boat lying on its side on the beach. 'I've had some good times in her,' he said, 'but no doubt she'll give pleasure to her next owner.'

Thea drew in a deep breath. She was almost afraid to ask.

'Moving on?' she queried hesitantly.

'On and upwards,' he replied on an exhilarated note. 'Thanks to you I've been offered a post in Mr Conan's team. It sure was a lucky day for me when I met you,' he went on earnestly, and then held his hand out for the bemused Thea to shake. 'Well, I'd better get back to the job, I guess. You won't be around here for much longer either, from what I hear,' he added, giving Thea a very knowing look. The next moment he had gone on his way, stopping to give her one last wave as he left the beach.

When he was out of sight, Thea turned back to her work and started to clear the till, her fingers automatically counted the notes, but her thoughts were far from her task.

If Marcus had not had time to pull Sam off his watchdog duty, then surely he had not had the time to contact Timothy? She shook her head bewilderedly. Nothing was making sense, and why should he bother about Timothy now? And just what had Timothy heard—and from whom? Marcus? Her lips folded. It must have been Marcus, no one else would have that kind of information.

Placing the cash and the notes in the canvas bag ready to take back to Mrs Welling, she gave a deep sigh. She felt like a bird who had just tasted freedom, only to find itself trapped in another net, and too tired this time to look for a way out.

She picked up the takings and the empty tray, then left the kiosk, locking the door behind her. Sam took the tray from her as he had done each day since his appearance and accompanied her back to Beach House, where he gave his usual soft, 'Night, missy,' and handed the tray back to her to take into the house.

The cool shower she took directly she reached the house helped to soothe her ruffled feelings, but did little to ease the ache in her heart. Why not marry the wretched man and be done with it? she asked herself wearily. He wasn't going to accept defeat, his pride wouldn't let him let her go. He had said as much in front of John Smythe yesterday, she thought, as she recalled his words when John had asked him if she was a philanthropist. 'Whatever she is, I'm hanging on to her,' he had said, and once again Thea felt that strong hand of his lightly caressing her bare waist as he held her close to him, and gave a light shudder at the recollection. He would show her no mercy once they were married, of that she was certain. He meant to make her pay for her audacity in jilting him.

Her hand stilled on the towel as she dried herself. Seven years had been his latest forecast before the rot set in their marriage, and considering his soured outlook on matrimony, it was quite a concession, she thought ironically. She remembered that she had said something that had amused him, and it was that that had brought the upgrading of his earlier forecast.

Seven years, she thought dreamily. She ought to get that down in writing before the marriage. There were many things she did not know about Marcus, but one thing she was certain of, he would not break his word.

The shrill ringing of the telephone in the hall brought her out of her dreamy musings, and she blinked in amazement. What was she doing even considering marrying Marcus? She must be off her head! Seven years indeed—more likely seven weeks before he told her to get out, if that long!

'Telephone, Thea. It's Pauline,' Mrs Welling called up the stairs to her.

'I won't be a minute,' she called back as she went into her bedroom and hastily dressed herself. It was odd that Pauline should call her at this time, just when she needed her, for Pauline might be able to help her find another job, but she hadn't expected to hear from her this week, since she knew John was on leave. Perhaps it was a good omen, she thought hopefully as she dashed down to answer the call.

'Hi!' Pauline's cheerful voice came over the wire. 'Feel like an evening out?' she queried lightly. 'Only John's cousin's on a visit, and I thought a foursome would be better than a threesome, if you see what I mean.'

'Well——' Thea replied doubtfully. She didn't much care for blind dates, even though whoever it was was John's cousin.

'Nothing to worry about,' Pauline assured her quickly. 'He's just got engaged to a girl back in the States. The only thing you'll have to worry about is being bored to death by a list of her virtues!'

Thea's chuckle gave the answer to this. 'Very well, then,' she replied. 'What time, and where?'

'We'll pick you up,' Pauline answered. 'Say, in about half an hour's time, how's that? Oh, and no need to dress up—well, nothing elaborate, that is, it's a sort of disco place we're going to called Dirty Dick's,' she added happily.

Thea's eyebrows rose at the name. 'Dirty Dick's,' she repeated. 'It wouldn't be in a cellar by any chance, would it?' she queried dryly.

It was Pauline's turn to chuckle. 'As a matter of fact, yes,' she replied. 'But the music's good, and they don't charge the earth for drinks. See you,' and she rang off.

'Oh, dear,' said Mrs Welling as Thea replaced the receiver, 'is that where Pauline's taking you? Only it wasn't quite the place to take a young lady in my day. You did say Dirty Dick's, didn't you, dear?' she persisted. 'Of course, times have changed since then,' she went on musingly, 'and it's probably quite respectable now.' She talked on slowly, but did not sound very convinced of this.

'Well, I don't suppose it was a disco then,' Thea replied with twinkling eyes, as she went back towards the stairs again to get ready for her evening out. 'Still, I know I can rely on you to bail me out if I fall foul of the law,' she added teasingly, and was rewarded by a deep chuckle from the old lady before she went back into the lounge.

CHAPTER TEN

THEA chose to wear a sleeveless cotton dress with a multi-floral pattern and wide flared skirt for the occasion, and carrying a cashmere cardigan over her arm, she was ready for her evening out.

John's cousin Paul was a quiet, unassuming young man whose attention half the time appeared to be elsewhere, and the reason was not hard to guess at—newly engaged young men's thoughts were usually with their beloveds, distance only serving to heighten their affection.

Pauline's grin and pressure on her arm as they left the car down one of the town's side streets and entered a very unprepossessing entrance to the club told Thea she was as glad to see her as she was to see Pauline, and Thea hoped to be able to snatch a few minutes alone with her to sound her out on future job prospects.

The lower they descended down the steps that led to the club, the darker it seemed to become, and Thea was reminded of Mrs Welling's comments on its past history. 'They've usually got a light halfway down the stairs,' Pauline remarked. 'I guess the bulb's gone; we must tell the doorkeeper, John, or someone might get hurt,' and she kept Thea close to her as they negotiated the last section towards a dimly lit door at the end of a small corridor in front of them, from which sounds of music could be heard.

The interior was no better illuminated than the stairs, Thea thought, as they entered the club, and John gave Paul instructions to find them a table somewhere while he waited to have a word with the doorkeeper about the stairs.

By the time they had found an unoccupied table, Thea's eyes had adjusted to the dim lighting, and she was able to study her surroundings during a brief lull between the dancing. The room was a cellar, even though a very large one, and apart from a few posters on the walls depicting scenes from old Chicago in the gun-running days, there were no other trappings, but the place was spotlessly clean, as were the chequered plastic cloths on the tables.

There were no waiters gliding unobtrusively between the tables here, and whatever beverage was required was collected from a makeshift bar at the end of the room. The whole effect was studiously informal and, judging by the press of customers, very popular.

As John had still not joined them, although he could be seen from where they sat, enjoying a chat with the doorkeeper, Paul elected to go and collect their drinks, and Thea saw a chance of snatching a quick word with Pauline. 'You wouldn't by any chance know——' was as far as she was able to get, as the dance music started up again, completely drowning Thea's query whether Pauline knew of any job vacancies.

'Any what?' shouted Pauline, trying to raise her voice against the steady pulsating beat of drums, and Thea raised her hand in a 'forget it' gesture, knowing it was hopeless trying to compete with the music.

So the evening progressed, and after Thea had got over her disappointment of not being able to have a word alone with Pauline, she quite enjoyed herself. The music was good, and although the dancing area was crowded there was such an atmosphere of friendliness and good humour around her, she was able to forget her troubles.

Another thought that had occurred to her during the evening was that Pauline would now be free for another fortnight as John was joining his ship that night, and there was nothing to stop her from seeing her on one of these evenings, and this thought had cheered her up considerably.

They were half-way through a popular dance number when the music suddenly stopped and an authoritative voice cut through the sudden silence. 'This is just a routine check and nothing to get alarmed about,' said a uniformed officer, moving towards the centre of the floor. 'We'll have some lights on for a start,' he ordered, and when this was complied with he turned back to the apprehensive dancers. 'It won't take long if you all co-operate. Would all with American citizenship move to the left, and the aliens to the right, with their passports ready if they have them with them.'

'Looks as if someone's skipped ship,' said John with a grin. 'It's stupid really, it never works. They won't get far without their passport, and the Purser's got that.'

Pauline gave a giggle and whispered to Thea, 'It's just like the movies, isn't it?' and started to pull her over to the line on the left where John had already stationed himself with Paul.

'Hold it,' said Thea, 'I'm an alien, remember?'

and went over to the other side of the room and joined a straggling line of not more than a dozen people.

Pauline hesitated for a second, then went over to join Thea. 'I'll vouch for you,' she offered. 'Have you got your passport with you?' she asked.

Thea pulled her shoulder-bag round in front of her and started to look for her passport, then suddenly her hands stilled in the search and she shook her head despondently. 'No, I haven't,' she said slowly, for she had just remembered where her passport was—Marcus had it. He had had to borrow it to claim Michael's estate for her. 'Mr Conan's got it,' she told Pauline bleakly, but did not explain further. 'It looks as if I'll need your help after all.'

Her bleak expression said more than words, for the old trapped feeling had come back to her with a vengeance. She hadn't been allowed to enjoy just this one evening without her previous involvement with Marcus coming out, as it surely would during the coming interview with the young police inspector who had stationed himself on her side of the queue.

When it came to Thea's turn to receive inspection, Pauline was not able to give the necessary aid, for when Thea explained that she did not have her passport with her, and when asked where her passport was, having to admit that it was not in her possession at all but in someone else's, she received a very suspicious look from the policeman, who hadn't liked the sound of that at all.

Pauline's quick, 'I can vouch for Miss John,' was totally ignored, much to her annoyance, and she contented herself with glaring at the policeman.

The next question was predictable, and there was no help for it but for Thea to give him Marcus's name, adding swiftly, 'My brother worked for him,' in the hope that this would explain everything.

By now Pauline had reached the end of her tether. It was bad enough being ignored, but she was not having Thea put through all this. 'Look, Jim Strawson,' she said, with a glint in her eyes. 'You know me, and I know you. If I say Miss John's okay, then she's okay. We'll get the passport for you tomorrow, how's that?' she challenged him belligerently.

The young inspector gave her a slightly embarrassed grin. 'I'm only doing my duty,' he said quickly, then reverted back to the official tone with, 'We shall have to contact Mr Conan to verify this,' and looked back at the weary Thea. 'Would you mind sitting over there, please, miss, until I get through the rest of this line-up.' He turned his attention back to the fuming Pauline. 'Why don't you go on home?' he suggested mildly. 'This might take some time. I'll see the young lady gets back home okay.'

Pauline was all set to argue the point, but John stepped in with, 'We've only an hour before I have to report back. Jim'll see Thea's okay, won't you, Jim?' he appealed to the policeman.

Thea could see John's point. It wasn't their fault that she didn't have her passport with her, and he had no wish to cross the authorities or risk losing his job by being late in reporting back to his ship. It wasn't a case of letting Thea down, but plain common sense.

Pauline gave Thea a helpless look. She was torn

between leaving with John or staying with Thea.

'It's all right, Pauline,' Thea reassured her hastily. 'Look, I'll give you a ring when I get back to Beach House, how's that?' she suggested.

During all this time Paul, who had wisely kept in the background, now half-heartedly suggested that he should stay with Thea, but John's sharp, 'And how are we to get back? We're using your car, remember?' put paid to this tentative offer, and Thea was very relieved about this. She couldn't blame Paul for not wanting to get involved either. He didn't know anything about her, and she might have been on Interpol's wanted list for all he knew!

Before they finally left, Pauline reminded Thea of her promise to ring her as soon as she got back to Beach House, and giving the policeman a final glare she allowed John to lead her away.

When they had gone, Thea felt utterly forlorn. When she had first checked in at the airport immigration desk in Miami on her way to St Thomas, she had been surprised to find herself classed as an alien. Foreigners, of course, were aliens, but somehow she hadn't thought the term applied to the English in America. Now she felt like an alien with a capital A, and miserably wondered what she was doing there anyway, so far from her native land.

The line on the left of the room had quickly dispersed, and it was obvious that there would be no more dancing that evening, as everyone had elected to leave as soon as they had been given the authority, and the large proportions of the room looked vast in the emptiness.

Thea found herself receiving several side glances from the few aliens still waiting in the queue. Some were sympathetic, and some just curious, and she took a deep breath of exasperation. It was Marcus's fault that she was in this embarrassing position. He ought to have known she would need her passport at some time or another, but as with other things where he was concerned, it simply hadn't occurred to him, she thought furiously.

When she recalled her parting jest to Mrs Welling that evening about not supposing she would need bailing out, she almost winced. She hadn't dreamt that her quip might backfire on her like this.

Her thoughts roamed on. If there was one good thing about what had happened that evening it was that she hadn't realised that Marcus still had her passport, and she could hardly book her passage home without it. Tomorrow she would ring him and request that he send it back to her, she told herself grimly.

It must have been only a quarter of an hour since Pauline had left, but to the waiting Thea it felt more like an hour. The queue of aliens had now dispersed, leaving Thea feeling even more isolated, and she wondered if they were having trouble locating Marcus. One swift glance at her watch told her that it was almost ten-thirty, and not really late—unless he was entertaining someone, she thought bitterly, and in that case he would be furious at being contacted on such a trivial matter as Thea John's passport.

For a moment she thought she had imagined the smooth, 'Well, well,' behind her, that sounded remarkably like Marcus's voice, but on turning round to meet his green mocking eyes, she was convinced of his presence.

She felt her heart leap at the sight of him, and again felt like throwing herself in his arms. She had been lost and now she had been found. It was a ridiculously childish feeling, and she was ashamed of it. She was not a child and refused to act like one, so she swallowed hard and took refuge in anger. 'There was no need for you to come out,' she snapped at him. 'All you had to do was to vouch for me, and say you had my passport.'

'There's gratitude for you,' drawled Marcus with raised brows. 'Here I **am**, rushing to your rescue, and all I get is three lashes of the whip!' He glanced around the now completely bare room. 'Did your escort desert you?' he asked deceptively mildly, but the tone of his voice said that he would like a few words with whoever it was.

'I hadn't an escort,' Thea bit back swiftly, then at Marcus's expression went on to correct that last statement. 'Not a special escort, that is. I came with a party, and there was no need for them to hang around. The inspector told me he would see I got back to Beach House.'

'Oh, I told them that wouldn't be necessary,' Marcus replied grandly. 'Are you ready?' he asked.

Thea stared back at him. 'Can we go?' she asked, and then realising what a silly question that had been, jumped up quickly and began to head for the door with Marcus's long strides easily keeping pace with her.

'I don't want you to go to that place again,' he said authoritatively, as he shut the car door on her and got into the car. 'Not that I think you will. I'm just telling you for the record.'

His dictatorial attitude annoyed Thea. She would

do exactly what she liked whether he liked it or not!
'I know it didn't used to have a good name,' she
said tartly, 'Mrs Welling said so, but that was a long
time ago, and things change, even she said that. Besides,' she added crossly, 'Pauline and John would
have looked after me. If I had had my passport with
me I could have left with them.' This reminded her
of what she was going to ask Marcus. 'Have you got
my passport?' she asked quickly.

Marcus's eyes left the road for a brief instant as he
glanced at her, then resumed to watch the road
ahead of them and gave a swift nod.

'Oh, good,' she breathed with relief.

'The place is all right,' he went on, completely
ignoring Thea's reference to her passport, 'it's the
characters who use it. The proprietors try to keep an
eye out for trouble, that's why they have a doorkeeper, but occasionally a few unwanted clients slip
through the net. Discos are the rage at the moment,
and the lowered lighting and spotlight colour beams
make an excellent cover for any amount of dubious
dealings.'

Thea could have told him that that wasn't what
the police were interested in that time, since she was
sure that John's guess had been nearer the mark,
and that someone had overstayed their shore leave,
but she said nothing. She was still annoyed over the
way he had sidestepped the passport issue.

When they reached Beach House, Marcus got out
and walked to the door with Thea, and this time she
wasn't going to be put off. 'May I please have my
passport?' she said, holding out her hand in hopeful
anticipation.

Marcus looked down at her outstretched hand

and put his large one over hers, his strong lean fingers gently caressing her palm and making shivers run down her spine at the small but intimate contact. She attempted to pull her hand away, but he held it fast. 'Not going anywhere, are you?' he asked silkily.

'As a matter of fact, yes,' Thea snapped, hating him for making her feel so helpless. 'Back to the U.K. when I've earned enough for my fare!'

His green eyes rested thoughtfully on her before he said, 'You're not broke, are you? What about Michael's money? Didn't the bank transfer it over to your account?' he demanded, again choosing to ignore her last remarks.

Thea blinked as the realisation suddenly hit her that she hadn't given a thought to that side of things. She had been so caught up with extricating herself from a loveless marriage with Marcus that everything else had taken second place. She drew in a deep breath. There would be enough to pay for her fare home. She was certain of it—and to think how worried she had been over seeking another job! Why, she could go tomorrow—or the next day—whenever she liked. A wave of relief washed over her until she remembered the passport. Without it she would get no further than the airport. 'I want that passport, please, Marcus,' she said firmly.

Marcus gave a loud sigh that didn't fool Thea for one moment. 'I'm afraid I haven't got it on me,' he said in a deceptively smooth voice.

'You said you had!' Thea accused him furiously.

'Did I?' he replied vaguely. 'You asked me if I had your passport and I said yes. I didn't say I had it on me,' he remonstrated gently.

Thea took a deep breath and tried counting to ten, but it didn't work. She wasn't to know if he was telling the truth or not, and there was nothing she could do about it. 'Well, send it over to me tomorrow,' was all she could say. 'If you don't, I shall be forced to go to the Consulate,' she threatened, showing him that she meant every word.

'Fighting mad?' Marcus queried casually, and Thea moved a step away from him in alarm. It was his way of telling her that she was asking for trouble in no uncertain way.

She eyed him warily before replying firmly, 'I am.'

He gave a deep chuckle at this and placed a quick kiss on her forehead. 'You're learning, sweetheart,' he said softly. 'As for your passport, I can do better than send it. I'll bring it to you Friday evening. I'm rather booked up until then,' and with an airy wave he walked back to his car, started up, and swept away from her bemused gaze.

He couldn't even allow her to bow out gracefully from the scene without making her await his authority, she thought bitterly as she went into the house and straight up to her room—she was in no mood for a chat with Mrs Welling. She had barely closed her bedroom door when she remembered her promise to Pauline, and with lagging steps she returned to the hall to make the call.

Her weariness must have shown in her face as she put the phone back on its receiver after assuring Pauline that everything was all right, and found Mrs Welling hovering at the door of the lounge. This time the old lady did not ask if everything was all right, as she had obviously heard what Thea had told Pauline. 'You go right on up, Thea,' she said soothingly. 'I can see you're tired. Tell me all about it tomorrow,' she suggested kindly, and Thea needed no second bidding and went to her room.

The first thing that came to mind when she awoke the following day was that she would be free to leave the island on Friday. The thought stayed with her while she showered and dressed, then went down to breakfast. She ought to have felt light-hearted and immensely relieved that the uncertainty was over, that she could now begin a new start to her life without fear for the future, but it was that part of it that was causing most of her misery. At least she had known what to expect if she stayed in St Thomas, but what could she look forward to if she returned to the U.K.? An even lonelier life than she would spend here, she thought dully, spending her days waiting for another Marcus to enter her life—only there wouldn't be another Marcus, there couldn't be. She swallowed as she sat down at the breakfast table. As it was all over now, at least she could admit it. She loved him desperately and there was no room in her heart for a replacement.

'Could you manage two eggs this morning, dear?' queried Mrs Welling as she entered the dining room, and Thea gave a swift shake of her head. She couldn't manage even toast, a cup of coffee was all she needed, but she did not say so, for she knew that her breakfast had already been cooked for her.

While she struggled with her egg and bacon, she tried to give a lighthearted account of what had ensued the previous evening, deliberately leaving Marcus's part out of it.

Mrs Welling's next question, however, proved

that she might not have bothered. 'Well, wasn't it a
good thing that Mr Conan knew where you were?'
she said, as she poured herself another cup of tea.

Thea, in the act of pushing her plate aside,
paused and stared at her. 'But he didn't,' she said,
'at least, not until the police rang through to get
him to verify my statement.'

'Oh, but he did, dear,' replied Mrs Welling comfortably. 'He rang here shortly after you had left
with Pauline, and I told him.'

Thea blinked as she digested this startling piece of
news, and the beginning of a suspicion filtered
through her mind. He couldn't have—could he? She
gave herself a mental shake. Of course he hadn't,
she told herself firmly; the very idea was ridiculous.

'You know, Thea, you're lucky,' commented Mrs
Welling cogitatingly, 'having a man like that watching out for you. You'll come to no harm with him
around, that's for sure,' she added happily.

This simple statement was about all Thea could
take at that time, and she closed her eyes. Mrs Welling didn't know the half of it. What if she told her
what was behind his pursuit of her? she wondered.
Would she be so sympathetic towards him then?

'Thea, are you feeling all right?' Mrs Welling
asked anxiously, as she studied Thea's set expression
and closed eyes.

Thea gave a short laugh that was not far short of
hysteria, then swallowed hastily in an effort to get
herself under control. She so badly wanted to talk to
someone, and her hopes of talking to Pauline had
come to nothing. Suddenly she had made her mind
up, and opened her eyes and fixed them on the
orange condiment set in the middle of the table.

'What if I told you that he asked me to marry him, and that I'd refused,' she said slowly but deliberately.

There was a short silence after this, and Thea, waiting to hear Mrs Welling's gasp of astonishment, felt a spurt of surprise when no such reaction came, and she looked at the old lady, and got another surprise when she saw that she was nodding and smiling to herself as if she had received confirmation of her own thoughts on the matter. 'And he won't take no for an answer,' she murmured, still busy with her own thoughts, then looked back at Thea. 'Why did you say no?' she asked curiously. 'And don't tell me you don't care for him, I've got eyes in my head, you know,' she added gently.

Thea bit hard on her lower lip, but couldn't stop the tears cascading down her cheeks and wiped them away with an impatient action. 'Because he doesn't love me,' she said quietly, seeing no point in lying. 'Oh, he's attracted to me, of course,' she stared dully at her hands twisted together in her lap. 'I don't know why, because I'm different, I suppose,' she added lamely. Her lovely eyes met Mrs Welling's sympathetic ones. 'He told me that himself,' her eyes fell quickly back to her hands. 'That was the only reason why he proposed, he said he knew I wouldn't go along with any other proposition.'

'Did he actually say that?' Mrs Welling asked gently, again surprising Thea, since she was not at all shocked and Thea felt that she ought to have been.

Thea nodded dully, and drew in a deep breath before she asked in a low voice, 'Would you have said yes, under those conditions?'

'As a matter of fact, I did,' replied Mrs Welling with a dreamy look on her face as she went back through the years. 'My, but it takes me back,' she said softly. 'My Charles was just like your Mr Conan. Oh, he hadn't his money, of course, or good education, but his thinking was just the same. Good-looking and a regular heartbreaker was my Charlie in those days. He could have had his pick of the girls in the neighbourhood, but for some reason he got stuck on me, and like you, I could never fathom it out. Just cussedness, I used to think, because I'd have none of him.' She broke off, and looked at Thea. 'I was scared of him, to tell the truth,' she admitted, then added, 'Well, not of him, but the thought of joining all those other girls he'd dropped when he lost interest in them,' she amended, and nodded slowly. 'Like your man, he wouldn't let go, hung on like a regular terrier, until he'd worn me down. I was in love with him, of course, always had been from the moment I'd met him, but I wasn't letting on.'

She sighed, and reached over for the teapot, testing it first to see if the brew was still drinkable, then poured herself out another cup when Thea refused to join her. 'Well, when he proposed, I accepted him. He hadn't proposed to any other woman, and that was good enough for me.' She took a sip of her tea. 'So I married him, because I loved him, but it didn't stop me worrying about the future. I'd got it into my head that one fine day he'd walk out on me.' She gave Thea a small smile. 'Divorces weren't easy to come by in those days—leastways, not for the likes of us—but there was nothing to stop him walking out of the door and not coming back.'

She was silent for a few seconds before she went on slowly, "There was one thing I didn't take into consideration, and that was that we were made for each other. Looks have nothing to do with it, or circumstances. If you were made for each other then you would marry. Charlie knew we belonged together right from the start. I didn't, until after we were married, then I knew. It's not something you can explain, it just happens,' she looked back at Thea. 'I think you'll find your man's like my Charlie. He'd no more admit that he loved me than fly to the moon. It's not always what they say that matters, but what they do.' She stared at the dark liquid in her cup. 'You know what? I think if a survey was conducted on all married folk, and the women answered truthfully, they would have to admit that their men never actually came out with the words "I love you", not without prompting, that is.' She looked suddenly up at the watching Thea. 'If that's all that's holding you back, then it isn't worth it, Thea. We all like to hear those words, of course, and I guess some have, but when it's the real thing, it's only a sort of icing on the cake, isn't it?' she asked earnestly.

Thea gave a swift nod, but did not say what she was thinking. She knew she belonged to Marcus, but Marcus belonged to no one but himself, she thought sadly.

'Remember that he didn't have all that happy a childhood,' Mrs Welling commented, accurately tuning in on Thea's thoughts. 'So he's soured on marriage. I guess that's what you're trying to tell me, isn't it?' she asked. 'Well, you listen to an old woman. Nothing in the world is plain sailing. You have to work at it, and you only get what you give, and that's even more important in marriage. I've a feeling that if his mother hadn't been so strong-willed the marriage would have been a happy one. It's give and take all the time, and knowing when to back down even though it hurts your pride.'

Thea gave another small nod at this. 'So you think I should marry him, do you?' she said quietly.

Mrs Welling smiled at her. 'It's my guess you won't get much peace until you do.' Then her expression sobered as she added, 'It's your life, Thea. Only you can make that decision. I can only remember how I felt at the time. I kept imagining what life would have been like without Charlie, and it didn't bear thinking about. I thought I was taking a gamble when I married him, but it turned out to be the wisest thing I ever did in my life.'

Mrs Welling's words stayed with Thea over the following few days, and she knew she would never forget them. They would haunt her through the years to come if she took that flight home, and turned her back on what might have been.

By the time Friday had come she had made up her mind to marry Marcus—if he should ask her again—and the thought that he might not made her turn cold. He knew she was thinking of leaving St Thomas, and surely he would make some attempt to stop her going—unless he had changed his mind, and her heart gave a painful lurch at this distinct possibility, visualising him handing her her passport and casually remarking that he hoped she had a good journey back.

While she waited for him to arrive that evening, she stayed in her bedroom, not wanting Mrs Well-

ing to see how strung up she was, for her nerves felt
close to breaking point, and if he should just hand
over her passport and then be on his way again, and
there was no reason why he shouldn't do just that,
since he had not made a definite date with her, she
simply did not know how she was going to face the
kindly old woman—or face anyone, come to that.

Although his car drew up with a sleek whisper of
tires, to Thea's heightened senses it sounded like an
explosion, and she made her way down the stairs
and towards the door, willing herself to take it easy,
but she could not prevent her hands clenching
themselves into small fists.

His casual 'Hi!' when she opened the door to him
made her heart beat faster, and at first she didn't
understand why his brows were raised at her appearance in just a sleeveless dress. 'You'll need a
cardigan,' he commented, 'and that precious article
no woman would be found dead without—i.e., a
handbag.'

It took a second for Thea to get his meaning, and
when it gradually got through to her that he
intended taking her out somewhere, she felt her
heart lift in hope, and muttering something about
not being a minute, she dashed back up to her room
to collect them.

As the car left Beach House, she tried not to stare
at his handsome profile or at his strong nicely
shaped hands that held the wheel of the powerful
car so effortlessly, and when he spoke to her she
almost jumped. 'I want your opinion on a place I've
found for John,' he said. 'He's decided to move over
here lock, stock and barrel.' He gave her a quick
sidewise look before he added, 'He'll trust your

judgment rather than mine in these matters.'

Thea swallowed hard. He was making sure that
the conversation kept on an even keel, she thought,
and in a way she was being used again. When she
had given her opinion she supposed that would be
the time when he would hand her her passport, with
a 'bon voyage' thrown in.

The drive was in the direction of Pirates' Cove,
but they turned off the main highway before they
reached the hotel and followed a winding track up a
hillside until a large white residence came into view.
Thea held her breath. Without going any further,
she knew that the view from the house would be
breathtaking, as it was in a commanding position on
the top of the hill it was built on.

The immaculate lawns that surrounded the
house, and the finely laid-out gardens beyond, en-
hanced the scene, and she wondered if Moira would
have the sense to appreciate the beauty of her surroundings.

Without even going into the house, Thea could
have said that the house and grounds were ideal, for
she simply couldn't see anyone turning it down, not
if they had the money to purchase it, that was, and
John Smythe certainly had.

Her heart was heavy as she followed Marcus into
the house, since she couldn't see the point of further
exploration. The place was large enough, if John
had entertaining in mind, and she could almost see
Moira standing at the top of the steps in front of the
house welcoming their guests.

As they went from one stately room to another,
the absence of furniture emphasising the proportions
of each room, Thea thought of Moira again, and

found herself envying her the task of furnishing this lovely house, particularly as there was no shortage of money in that direction.

The house consisted of four storeys, the ground floor containing the usual large lounge, dining room, study and what could have been a small sitting room. Then there were the domestic quarters, an ample sized kitchen, a butler's pantry, and two reasonable sized rooms, probably used by the staff as a dining room and lounge.

The second floor contained the master bedroom, and three more bedrooms, a luxurious bathroom in turquoise and black tiling, and separate shower unit. The bath itself was set in the floor in the middle of the room in the shape of a seashell, and looked like a miniature swimming pool to Thea's bemused gaze. If Moira didn't appreciate the gardens, she would certainly appreciate that, she thought ironically, as they went up to the third floor.

By the time they had got through the third floor that contained three more bedrooms, and to Thea's embarrassment, a nursery, she felt she had taken enough punishment without being reminded of a certain conversation she had had with Moira about children.

Marcus had been remarkably quiet during the inspection, as if letting Thea make up her own mind on the suitability of the house for John, and she thought he was probably hoping she would hurry her decision so that he could drop her back at Beach House again, and out of his life.

'I don't think it's necessary to see any more,' she said quickly, as Marcus turned towards the stairs leading to the fourth floor. 'You can tell John that it's

a beautiful house,' and coloured as she felt his
searching eyes on her face. 'Well, not in those words,
of course,' she amended hastily. 'Just say that I
approve of your choice.'

'There's not much more to see,' Marcus replied
mildly, 'only a few more rooms, but the view's
worth it.' He stood determinedly by the stairs waiting for Thea to go ahead of him.

Thea had no choice but to lead the way to the
upper storey. Each of the front rooms had had a
lovely view, and she had purposely refrained from
lingering at the windows. She could well imagine
the splendid vista shown from the upper floor, and
could see no reason for his insistence on showing it
to her.

There were four bedrooms on this floor, and they
were probably the staff rooms, for they were of smaller dimensions than the lower rooms. Two faced the
front of the house, and it was in the larger of the two
that Marcus drew Thea's attention to the window
and the view beyond.

She stood by his side and looked out on the glori-
ous scene before them. She wasn't sure which bay
they were looking over, but thought it was probably
Magens Bay. The sun had begun its descent and the
bright orange rays fanned the bay and were reflected in the water, now a dark velvety blue.

It was breathtakingly beautiful and a sight that
Thea knew she would never forget in the long lonely
days ahead of her. She had seen other sunsets on the
island, but this one was special because of the silent
man by her side. The man she loved so much, and
who would shortly grant her her ticket to freedom, a
freedom she no longer wanted.

Her breath caught in her throat as the sun slipped even further below the skyline. Why couldn't she tell him how she felt?—plead with him, tell him that she loved him, and that she would marry him, if only he would ask her again. She swallowed. Marcus hadn't bothered to see her even once after she had told him that she was leaving the island, and had only arranged to see her that evening to bring her her passport. She could have been catching a late night flight for all he knew, she thought bitterly—or cared, but at least he had been honest about that, and she could blame no one but herself for her unhappiness.

'I hope the electricity isn't cut off,' she said curtly, in an effort to break the spell of utter despondency that threatened to engulf her. 'It will be dark in a moment, and we've three flights to negotiate, remember?' she added waspishly, and gave a gasp of indignation as she felt Marcus's arm steal around her waist and draw her near him. So that was what this little expedition was all about, she thought bitterly; he didn't intend to waste any opportunity before she left, and she struggled to extricate herself.

'Shame on you!' said Marcus with a trace of amusement in his voice. 'Thinking of things like that, at a time like this! I prefer starlight, it's more appropriate for the occasion.'

'It's not an occasion,' Thea snapped back, still frantically trying to free herself and feeling the old weakness steal over her senses at his nearness.

To her surprise he released her, and stood gazing out at the darkening landscape where the first of the evening stars were appearing. 'When do you plan to leave?' he asked her, in a casual voice as if not really interested but asking for politeness' sake.

'As soon as possible,' Thea got out on a grating note. 'Now, please can we go?' she demanded.

'So you like the house,' Marcus commented, ignoring her request. 'What if I told you it could be yours?' He looked at her. 'And mine,' he added significantly.

Thea felt a lump gathering in her throat. If he was playing with her—She swallowed. 'I thought you said it was for John,' she answered in a low voice, not knowing what else to say. She couldn't believe that he could be so cruel as to try and bait her like that.

'So I'm giving you first refusal,' he replied harshly. 'I closed the deal on this place the morning after we got engaged. I'd planned to bring you out here that evening.'

Thea held her breath, then closed her eyes. He had said nothing of this before, and still she was finding it hard to believe. 'Is that true?' she whispered, her eyes searching through the shadows on his face. 'Be fair, Marcus—don't play with me!'

'Play with you?' he replied savagely. 'What the hell do you think you were doing with me? Was it fair of you to walk into my life, turn it upside down, and calmly walk out again? No, I'm not playing. This is for real, and you'd better believe it. I want your answer now, and it had better be the right one this time,' he warned her harshly. 'I don't fancy chasing you half across the world, but I will if there's no other way. You might just as well say yes, and be done with it,' he threatened.

Thea's whole being suddenly flooded with light. She knew now what Mrs Welling had meant when she had said that it wasn't necessary for a man to actually say the words 'I love you'. There were other words that said the same thing, and she had just heard them. She threw herself into his arms and wrapped her arms around his lean waist, burying her head in his strong chest. 'I thought——' she swallowed, 'I thought you'd never ask me to marry you again. I was so unhappy,' her breath caught in a sob. 'I do love you, Marcus. I always have.'

'Tell me something I don't know,' Marcus replied gruffly, gently raising her head from his shoulder and making her look at him. 'I knew that, at least. What I couldn't figure out was what got into you. I thought you'd suddenly got scared of committing yourself for life, and that reminded me of a quarrel between my father and mother. I was supposed to be asleep, but how they expected me to sleep through that racket, and through all the other rows they had, is beyond me.' His lips gently teased the corners of her soft mouth. 'I remember my mother shouting that they should have been lovers, not man and wife—she said she felt she had a halter round her neck, and they oughtn't to have had a child, because now they were trapped together,' his lips now covered hers, and Thea was lost in the magical world of love.

There was so much she wanted to tell him, so much she could now understand, but for the moment it was enough to feel his arms around her and his hard demanding lips on hers, and when he gently put her away from him a short while later, she knew the reason for that too. 'Marcus, I want you to promise me something,' she said, not looking at him but out at the starlit night beyond.

'When——' she hesitated, and began again, a little more firmly this time, for this was something that she wanted him to understand right from the start. 'When it's over, when you feel——' she swallowed, 'well, you know what I mean. I want to stay on here, that's if you can afford it,' she added hastily, 'and I understand about your not wanting children. I didn't before, but I do now.' Her voice broke slightly, as she added, 'It will be enough for me to have you with me for as long as you want me.'

She heard his quick inward gasp and the next minute he had swept her into his arms again and was kissing her with a fierce intensity as if she had just said goodbye to him, and he couldn't bear to let her go. 'I don't want to hear you ever say anything like that again, do you hear?' he said savagely, his hold on her tightening to a suffocating clamp on her slight figure. 'Sure, I was fool enough once to think that I wouldn't hang on to you, as my mother thought my father had done, or to saddle you with a child, but we'll get this straight right from the start. I'm taking out a ninety-nine-year lease on you, honey, and I don't back losers. As for kids,' his lips roamed her creamy throat, 'one's not enough. I'm not having a child of mine knowing the loneliness I went through—besides,' he added autocratically, 'they'll be my surety for our future, and there'll be no way out for you.'

Thea gave a contented sigh, and kissed his strong jawline. Her cup of happiness was full, but woman-like she couldn't resist asking about Sapphire, although by now she was sure that Moira had told the truth about his relationship with her. She pulled herself gently out of his arms and looked at him searchingly. 'And Sapphire, Marcus? Was it you that sent her to the hotel?' she asked, her lovely eyes asking the question she really needed assurance on.

Marcus pulled her back into his arms again before he replied against her hair, 'I wondered when we were going to get around to that,' and there was a trace of amusement in his voice. 'I needed a reason to see you. I also needed to know if I'd been wrong about you. I was pretty sure I'd got you before—before you chucked that bombshell at me, that was.'

Thea's head jerked up at this. 'You tried to make me jealous of her!' she said indignantly, then instantly relented, for she felt sorry for Sapphire, and nestled against him again. 'I was jealous, Marcus,' she confessed softly. 'I hated you both.'

There was a low chuckle from Marcus at this. 'So I gathered,' he replied. 'That was obvious by the way you hared out of the job.'

'Think you'll be ready in a week?' Marcus asked her a short while later in a voice that was beginning to show a certain amount of strain, and when she replied softly that she was 'ready' now, he gave a groan. 'Don't tempt me, sweetheart. Why do you think I kept my distance from you all this time?' and he pushed her gently away from him. 'So, a week it is,' he said softly. 'I'm not risking waiting for all the trappings, you can have that later if you want. I'm getting a special licence and we'll be married from the hotel. A six-week honeymoon in the U.K. should be long enough for the decorators to get busy in here and have it ready for our return.'

'Blue and gold,' Thea murmured dreamily, as she drifted back into his arms again.

'Blue and what?' queried Marcus, determinedly holding her away from him again, and trying to get the gist of her thinking.

'I was just furnishing our lounge, darling,' she said, still in that dreamy voice. 'And green and gold for the dining-room. For the nursery, pink and gold—or blue and gold—a bit of both, I think——' was as far as Marcus allowed her to get before he gave another groan, and swept her back into his arms again.